ASSIGNMENT NEW YORK

Borgo Press Books by E. C. TUBB

ASSIGNMENT NEW YORK

A MIKE LANTRY CLASSIC CRIME NOVEL

E. C. TUBB

THE BORGO PRESS
MMXIII

ASSIGNMENT NEW YORK

Special thanks to Heather and Dave Datta for scanning this book.

FIRST BORGO PRESS EDITION

Published by Wildside Press LLC

www.wildsidebooks.com

DEDICATION

For Gary Lovisi

CONTENTS

INTRODUCTION
by Philip Harbottle

E. C. Tubb is a name instantly recognized by readers of science fiction, but his novels in other genres are not nearly so well known, chiefly because they were first published under pseudonyms. This non-sf output comprised one historical foreign legion novel, eleven westerns, the 'Atilus the Gladiator' ancient Rome trilogy, and a solitary detective novel, *Assignment New York*.

Some readers may be surprised that Tubb published a detective novel—and after reading it may be surprised that he did not published many more! To be strictly accurate, he *has* published numerous short stories with a strong detective fiction element—but always within the framework of science fiction. Additionally, many of his 'Dumarest' sf novels have strong mystery elements, but it is in his shorter sf stories that he comes closest to simon-pure detective fiction, in such stories as 'Nonentity' (*Authentic*, 1955) 'Reluctant Farmer' (*Nebula*, 1956), and 'The Ming Vase' (*Analog*, 1963). The latter story, particularly, is constructed like a Swiss watch.

In Tubb's stories, every action and reaction cannot just be allowed to happen fortuitously: it must have a logical reason. Thus, if the hero is caught in an ambush and shot at by the villain, it is not enough for the villain to simply miss (as miss he must to enable the story to continue!). Tubb would seek to explain how the hero had heard the click of the trigger being pulled back, or caught a gleam of light reflected from the barrel of a weapon, etc.—something that instinctively causes the hero to dodge aside at the last moment. His work is consistently logical, and the seeds of any devices to be used later are always planted beforehand—there is no *deus ex machina*. In other words, Tubb's fiction consistently employs the precise techniques of the best writers of detective fiction. This fact prompted me to ask the author why he had not written other detective novels.

He told me:

> "In all stories logical development is important, but in the detective novel it is *essential*. To write one with any degree of precision, it is necessary to know what's going to happen next, and what the ending will be. Not the simplest thing if (as 1 do!) you find it hard to plot in advance.
>
> "Usually my stories, once started, tended to write themselves. Situations grew from situations and, when writing sf and westerns, there was plenty of movement and action to

provide development. I could have started a detective novel easily enough, but then would have come the necessity of determining the plot, deciding who the villain should be, the motive, means, and opportunity worked out in a fair and logical fashion. As an analogy, to plot a good detective novel is like deciding, in advance, all the moves of an intricate game of chess. I found it a difficult thing to do.

"Short stories could be given a mystery or criminal element, as in 'The Ming Vase', which your instance shows, but to write a detective story, as a detective story, was too painful an exercise."

How then did Tubb come to construct such an elaborate story as *Assignment New York*, a book that works on two different levels? Beginning as a traditional tough private eye investigation, with a two-fisted shamus who knows how to take punishment and dish it out as well, it becomes seamlessly integrated into a cerebral detective mystery. The tangled narrative strands are neatly tied into a pleasing knot before Tubb triumphantly unveils them in the classic tradition of the detective story.

The character of Mike Lantry, his private eye narrator, is undoubtedly modelled from the classic Raymond Chandler mould—a hard-drinking cynical private eye, slightly down at heel, but with a fine sense of chivalry and compassion. The opening plot-line, involving the Colonel and his missing daughter, is reminiscent of Chandler's *The Big Sleep*, but once the story gets underway, Tubb's plotting and writing become increasingly original.

Tubb explained to me that at first, *Assignment New York* was written in his usual style at that time, which was not to do too much plotting in advance, but to simply let the story and characters flow. But Tubb came to the end of the story without having identified the murderer! "I simply couldn't manage to solve the given problem before running out of space!" (In the 1950s, publishers limited the length of their novels to around 40,000 words.) There was nothing for it but for Tubb to go back and rewrite his ms., writing in the clues and developing motives, etc. The antithesis to the normal method of writing a detective novel! A difficult feat, and one reason why Tubb chose not to write another detective novel. But there were other reasons.

Tubb had created Mike Lantry at his publisher's request, to launch a new 'Mystery Series' of American private eye novels. But shortly thereafter, Tubb had been obliged to sever his connections with the publisher, John Spencer Ltd.:

He told me:

> "At the time Spencer's were a low-pay market and I was about to be appointed as the editor of *Authentic Science Fiction*. I was also doing a full-time job, which only left the evenings and weekends free. Weekends meaning half-day Saturday and all day Sunday, during which time I tried to hit higher paying markets.

I informed Spencer's that I could not submit any further material for them, as I was concentrating on sf, which offered a wider (and more lucrative) field."

But the character of Mike Lantry did not die after just one book. The canny publishers quickly commissioned another of their writers, Anthony A. Glynn, to continue his adventures. Glynn's book was entitled *A Gunman Close Behind*, and this title is also now available in a new Borgo edition. Spencer's private eye series continued under other writers, most notably John Glasby, who created his own private eye, Johnny Merak. In later years Glasby would revive his character for another U.K. publisher for a whole series of Merak novels. Borgo Press will also be reprinting these fine novels in the U.S. for the first time, beginning with *Rackets, Inc.*

Tubb's decision not to continue with detective novels is surely a matter for regret. But at least we can enjoy this single example of his talent. And what's more, Borgo Press have been publishing new collections of Tubb's science fiction mystery and detective short stories, which to date include *The Wager*, *The Ming Vase*, *The Wonderful Day*, *Enemy of the State*, and *Only One Winner*. Also available from Borgo are his foreign legion novel, *Sands of Destiny*, and his Ancient Rome trilogy, *Atilus the Slave*, *Atilus the Gladiator*, and *Atilus the Lanista..* A feast for all lovers of great genre fiction!

CHAPTER ONE

If you're ever in New York, take a walk down Madison Avenue and stop outside Delhany's jewellery store. Turn towards the street, lift up your eyes and, five storeys above the sidewalk, you'll see a big sign:

WORLD-WIDE INVESTIGATIONS

There's a smaller sign on the ground level, and an elevator will take you up to a suite of offices. There's a reception room with a secretary who handles the casual trade. There are offices for consultations, a switchboard, a nest of filing cabinets, and a complete set of law books. There's a lot of staff too, and the general impression is that World-Wide is a pretty busy concern.

It is too.

But it wasn't always like that. There was a time when the agency comprised one operative who lived with his gun in his second-best suit and dodged more debt collectors than customers. That was a long time ago now, before the agency grew respectable and opened offices in all the major cities, when a case was a case and had to be attended to personally or not at all.

The boss had a pretty rough time of it then, but when success came, it came fast, and Mike Lantry rode the wave upwards.

I should know.

I'm Mike Lantry.

I stood outside Delhany's and stared at the big sign the way I always do when I'm walking to the office. It was growing dark and, as I watched, the time-switch tripped the current so that it flamed with bright red neon. The light tinged the dusk with the colour of blood, and for some reason I felt all nostalgic inside. Delhany came out to fix his shutters and nodded to me.

'Evening, Mike.'

'Evening.' I smiled as I said it. Delhany, despite outward appearances, handled a fortune in cut and uncut stones, dealing mostly with collectors and the trade. He, like me, had come up the hard way and that, if nothing else, gave us something in common. He nodded towards the sign.

'Sure looks good, Mike. Busy?'

'As ever.'

'Cagey?' He shrugged. 'I don't blame you; what a man doesn't know he can't spill.' He shivered as the wind cut down the avenue. 'It's going to be a stinking night, Mike. Winter's come early this year.' He blew on his hands, tested his shutters, and nodded good night. I nodded back, then looked at the sign again. It was still new enough to be worth looking at, but old enough so that I didn't have to worry whether or not I could pay for it.

Those days were a long way behind me now.

A second blast cut down the avenue, whipping scraps of paper out of the gutter and sending them spinning down the sidewalk. I shivered, not with cold, and hunched my shoulders beneath my gabardine. Memories perhaps? I didn't know and didn't stop to find out.

Sam, the elevator boy, nodded to me as he opened his cage and took me up to the offices. He didn't speak much, which was one of the reasons I employed him, but he didn't miss much, either. He let me out, and Lucy, my blonde, outwardly dumb but inwardly shrewd secretary, paused in the act of struggling into her coat.

'Mike! Something up?'

'Relax.' I stopped her taking off her coat and getting ready for work again. In a business like mine the clock doesn't have much meaning. You work when you can and rest when you're able, and if a case comes up in the middle of the night, you take it. Any case, anytime, anywhere, the one thing each and every employee has drilled and drilled into them.

'Westcote phoned through from London,' said Lucy. She still made no effort to go home. 'The Carruthers case is finished: the son had been passing forged cheques and trying to blame the maid. He said that he'd tied it up and that the old man was grateful.'

I nodded.

'Lambert wired from Paris, he thinks that he might have a lead on the Hammond emeralds. Should he follow it up?'

I nodded.

'There're more reports from Rio; López thinks that he might be on the trail of a smuggling racket.'

'Aliens?'

'He thinks so.' Lucy looked at me. 'Should I inform the Immigration Authorities?'

'I'll drop Inspector Cormay a hint,' I said. 'Tell López to keep his mind on his own work. The smuggling of illegal immigrants is Government business, not ours. Did you hear from Tokyo?'

'Report negative.'

'Berlin?'

'Case closed.'

'Rome?'

'Developments awaited.'

'In other words, everything is under control?'

'That's about it, chief.' I don't like being called chief and Lucy knows it, but we've known each other long enough for her to get away with it—sometimes. I picked up her purse and thrust it into her hand.

'Right. Beat it now and catch up on your beauty sleep. Is the night staff all in?'

'Yes.' She hesitated, sensing in the way that some women have, that something was wrong. 'What's the matter, Mike? Why have you come back this late?'

'No reason,' I said, and it was the truth. 'Just got to feeling restless, you know the way it is, and thought that I'd come back and sit awhile.' I pushed her towards the door. 'Get off now and enjoy yourself.'

'Sure.' She hesitated by the door. 'If you should need

me, you know where to find me.'

'I won't need you,' I said. 'I told you that there's nothing up, just that I got to feeling restless and thought that I'd clear up a few things. Now beat it!'

'Restless,' she sniffed. 'What you need is a wife and a houseful of children, they'd cure you. Why you haven't—'

I interrupted before she could get all sentimental, taking her arm and leading her almost to the elevator.

'Good night, Lucy, and don't come back until morning.'

'Good night,' she said and started to say something else. The clang of the doors drowned her words, and I made my way back into the office.

Into the inner office, that is, the one where I sit when I'm sitting, which isn't too often. It had grown quite dark by now, the wind was carrying more than a hint of rain, and it was a foul night of early winter. I stood by the window looking out into the avenue and, in the bright red of the neon sign, the gutters seemed to be running with blood.

I shrugged, annoyed at myself for my own imagination and, returning to the desk, opened the bottom drawer and reached for the Scotch.

I always keep Scotch in the bottom drawer. Not because I think it smart to drink, but because too often a slug of Scotch was the only meal I could afford, and because sometimes it did more than replace a lost night's sleep. I still keep it, not so much for myself now, as for the occasional client on the verge of breakdown, or for moments when, despite all the neon and offices, the secretaries and operators scattered all over the world, I remembered what I was and what I had been.

Better Scotch, of course, the same as the better suits, better offices, better car, and almost everything else.

But not better service.

I savoured the Scotch and was deciding whether or not to take a second drink, when the intercom buzzed and a voice came from the speaker.

'Mike?'

'Yes?'

'Heard that you'd come in.' Berson sounded tired. 'I've just reported back from L.A. Want I should see you?'

I thought about it, smiling a little as I stared down at my glass. Good old Berson, always reliable—to do the wrong thing. I'd sent him out to chase a missing husband and he'd probably frightened the guy to death or straight back to his wife, which wasn't what she'd wanted. She wanted a divorce and big alimony.

'Not tonight, Pug. Check in tomorrow.'

'But this is important, Mike. That guy ran like a rabbit and I think he headed straight back to his wife.'

'He did,' I said. 'Forget it. We found him for her, didn't we?'

'That's right.' Pug sounded pleased. 'Smart work, eh? I handled that one well, didn't I?'

'You did.' Useless to tell him that on every job he went on I had to send a man to cover him. Pug was all muscle and little brain, but what he lacked in intelligence he made up for in loyalty. I'd saved him from a frame and he followed me like a dog. 'Get some rest now and check in tomorrow. 'Night.'

I switched off and stared down at my desk. There was some mail, an airmail letter marked personal, and I opened it to stare at a shiny photograph of a man and woman with a couple of kids. I turned it over, but it wasn't necessary for me to read the inscription.

Sight of the letter made me remember the past, way back to where, almost, it had all begun. Outside, the wind hammered against the windows and that reminded me too. Years ago now, way back when I rented a cheap room and lived on the thin edge of debt, which is the penalty of any man who tries to make his own way in an overcrowded racket.

I stared at the photograph and sipped the Scotch. I felt tense, expectant, all keyed up, as if something was about to happen but I didn't know what. I'd felt like that before, and I didn't like it.

I rose and stared out of the windows again: still rain, still winds, still the red light making the gutters full of blood. I shivered. Different place, different building, but the same weather.

I crossed to the desk, and the faces of the couple smiled up at me.

Susan and Marvin. Boy and girl. Married now and with a couple of kids. I wondered whether the Colonel was still alive.

Thinking of him triggered something in my mind,

and I crossed to a green metal filing cabinet set against one wall. It was filled with neat, bound, typed pages. Some thick, some thin, but all with one thing in common. They were cases, some clean, some dirty, some, a very few, marked as unsolved. I let my finger run over them until I found the one I wanted. It was among the first, and I took it out and carried it back to my desk.

I was still tense, still expectant, but I just couldn't sit there and wait. So I opened the case and began to read, and as I read I went back...back...back to another night in another office where I sat waiting—and alone.

CHAPTER TWO

From where I sat at the desk, I could see the black marks of my name lettered on the frosted glass panel of the door. They were peeling flaked, but even in reverse I could figure out what they said and what the smaller lettering beneath them was supposed to say. Private Investigator. Me. An agency of one man in a crummy office, ready and willing to take care of all the troubles of the world.

Sight of the lettering reminded me of the rent I hadn't paid and the money I hoped to earn that night.

Midnight, the Colonel had said. Midnight to discuss a matter of the utmost privacy and desperate urgency. I discounted them both; trouble, no matter of what kind, is always desperate and urgent to the one who has it.

I rose and looked out of the window. Through the dirt I could see the rain and through the rain the lights looked fuzzy, as if they had lost their form and shape. A gust of wind pressed against the dirty panes, cold wind, bitter, heavy, with a hint of the coming snow.

It was a night to be indoors.

I thought so, and the sight of a few late pedestrians hurrying along the sidewalk, their collars turned high against the rain and hats low against the wind, made me certain of it. I stood staring at the snaggle-toothed skyline of New York, and the too-bright neon of Broadway shone from the low clouds as if half the city was burning.

An illuminated clock on a warehouse had both hands together as it pointed upwards in mechanical prayer.

Midnight.

The Colonel was late.

I sighed and lit a cigarette, sucking the smoke deep into my lungs and letting it plume against the glass of the window in swirling clouds of blue and grey. The smoke clouded the pane and I rubbed it, wiping a patch clear, then paused to stare at my reflection.

A face, two eyes, two ears, a nose, a mouth, a chin. Just a face topped with thick, slightly curly black hair. A face that had looked at the world with grey eyes for thirty years now, not a handsome one, not an ugly one, just a face, a mask for what went on within my skull. A thin scar puckered the cheek on the left side. One ear had a slight notch, a relic of my early days when the bullets fired had been with Government licence, and my lips seemed to have thinned a little and tended towards a downward curve.

I wondered if my mother would still have known me had she been alive.

I knew my father wouldn't have.

I shrugged and dragged at the cigarette, trying to find in the smoke some anodyne for the pressure I could feel building up inside of me. I had been idle too long and, unless I got a case soon, I'd join the ranks of those who accepted discipline for a steady wage.

So I stood and smoked and thought, and the flashing lights of the city painted the wet streets with changing tides of red and orange, green and amber, while the dim shapes beneath me hurried through the bitter wind.

I was still standing there when the limousine drew to a halt at the kerb below.

It was a long, smoothly-finished job, glittering with chromium and polish, looking like some huge, hard-shelled beetle as it rested on the street ten storeys below. A man slipped from the driver's seat, slamming the door behind him as, head down, he ran towards the building. Almost at once the harsh sound of the buzzer echoed around my ears.

I pressed the button releasing the night lock on the street door and, sitting down at my desk, waited for whoever it was to enter the office.

He was young, neatly dressed in chauffeur's black, his peaked cap throwing his eyes in shadow, and the close-fitting uniform didn't hurt his chest and shoulders one little bit.

'Mr. Lantry?'

'Yes.'

'Mr. Mike Lantry?' His voice was smooth and even, the schooled tones of a servant, a professional man, or a confidence trickster making his play. I nodded impatiently.

'That's right. What do you want?'

'Will you come with me, please.'

I didn't move. I stared at him, the cigarette between my fingers sending up a thin coil of smoke. After a time he realised that I was waiting for him to speak.

'My employer, the Colonel, is waiting in the car,' he said irritably. 'He wants to see you.'

'So what?'

'So you'd better do as he wants.' The mask had slipped a little, the voice lost some of its careful schooling and, in the shadow of the visored cap, his eyes glinted with a mingling of rage and contempt. I shrugged.

'He's going to be awfully disappointed. Go back and tell him that, if he wants to see me, he knows where to find me.'

'You refuse to come?'

'I refuse to obey the orders of any dressed-up lackey,' I said evenly, and something within me smiled at the expression on his face. 'Go back to your boss and tell him that.'

'You know who he is?' He couldn't seem to understand why I wasn't fawning at his heels. 'Colonel Geeson is a very rich man. Now, will you come?'

'No.' Deliberately I dropped the cigarette and crushed it beneath my heel. 'I'm different from you, buster. I haven't sold myself to ten million dollars, and I don't have to jump when he gives the orders.'

'Why, you stinking shamus!' The mask had slipped all the way now and naked rage glared at me from the shadow of the visor. 'If he wanted to he could buy a dozen just like you from any store. Who the hell do you think you are?'

'A man,' I said grimly. I got up from the desk and stepped towards him. 'Now get out of here and tell your personal god that I'm waiting to see him as arranged.' I stared at him. 'Better hurry, sonny: your nice, clean boots might get all dirty.'

He swung at me then, a wild, rage-dictated blow at my face, and I felt the wind of its passing as I swayed back. I didn't mind the blow, I'd asked for it; what I didn't like was the way his boot swept up towards my groin.

That made me annoyed.

I twisted, letting the heavy boot injure air as it slipped up the side of my thigh, then grabbed it as it reached the top of its swing. I twisted, swivelling the toecap around the heel, and he yelled as he threw himself in the direction of the rotation. He was smart, at that; if he hadn't, I'd have dislocated his hip. I smiled as his face smacked against the floor.

I would have let him alone then, let him limp back downstairs with a sore ankle and a sore nose, but he made the mistake of going for a gun.

I caught the glitter of it as it swung towards me, and I kicked at it. It fell from his hand, skittering towards a corner, and he threw himself after it. I trod on his hand just as he reached the butt.

'Cut it out,' I snapped. 'You're getting your uniform all dirty.'

He swore and clawed at me with his free hand. I stepped back and, as he tried to grab the gun, I swung my foot against the joint of his jaw. He sighed, his head jerking back, then sagged as he collapsed on the floor.

I picked up the gun, a .38 automatic, and poised it in my hand. It was a cheap, nickel-plated job, nothing special and probably as erratic as hell, but at close quarters it could kill a man just as surely as the most expensive hand-weapon ever made. I slipped out the magazine, thumbed the cartridges onto the desk, then jerked the slide to expel the one in the chamber. Releasing the slide, I threw the empty weapon down beside the sleeping man. Lighting a cigarette, I swept the cartridges into a drawer, then sat down on the edge of the desk, frowning at the unconscious figure on the floor.

I was still staring when the door opened and a man walked into the office.

He was an old man, tired, his face bearing the stamp of a lifetime of years. He stood, wheezing a little, leaning heavily on a snake-wood cane. His clothes were good, his soft hat probably cost more than I owed; his shoes were the kind which had their own last. Gold gleamed from his wrist, his cuffs, his fingers, and his teeth. He looked at me, then at the sleeping beauty, then at me again.

'Yours?' I blew smoke towards the chauffeur, and raised my eyebrows. He nodded.

'What happened?' His voice was a dry whisper, sounding like the rustle of dead leaves as they rubbed together when driven by the wind.

'He and I had a difference of opinion,' I said casually. 'I won.'

'Get him out of here, Mr. Lantry.'

'You know me?' I nodded. 'And you must be Colonel Geeson.'

He nodded and slumped into the customer's chair. I went across to the water cooler and filled a paper cup. I threw water and cup into the chauffeur's face. It didn't seem to do any good, so I picked up his feet and dragged him out of the office and into the corridor outside. It was cold out there, and dark, a good place to sleep. I picked up the empty gun and threw it beside him, then returned to my desk.

The old man stared at me, watching with his cold, snake-like eyes, and I sighed as I sat down and lit a cigarette.

'Why didn't you come when I sent for you?' he demanded.

'You,' I reminded him, 'stated that you would be coming to see me on private and urgent business. It's that difficult, the privacy I mean, with a chauffeur present?'

'The driving compartment is sealed,' he said absently. 'Was that your only reason?'

'Perhaps.'

'Or was it to impress me with your independence?' He stared at me with his glittering eyes. 'Arrogance isn't independence, Mr. Lantry.'

'A man values what he wants,' I said. 'If he values it enough, he will go and get it. Also,' I dragged at the cigarette, 'if you'd have wanted to meet me in your car you could have said so.'

'Caution.' He nodded. 'I was told that you were a cautious man.'

'By whom?'

'By the man who recommended that I should see you.' He obviously wasn't going to give me the name and I was tired of playing games. I got down to business.

'Well, what can I do for you?'

'You can help me,' he whispered, and something seemed to relax deep inside of him. I'd seen it before, that relaxation. It's always nice to know that you've got someone to do your worrying for you, especially when you've got the money to pay for it. 'You see, Lantry, it's my wife. She—'

'Hold it.' I pulled a scratch-pad towards me and made some pothooks. 'Let's start at the beginning. You're Colonel Geeson, you have a big house on Lower Manhattan, and a permanent penthouse off Fifth Avenue. You also own ten million dollars.'

'That is correct.' He didn't show his surprise at my knowing his business. Almost everybody would know that.

'Good. Now who is the boy-scout?'

'My chauffeur? Marvin. Peter Marvin, a nice boy, Harvard, I think.' He frowned as if that were of no importance.

'Been with you long?'

'Three years.' He shifted as though he found the chair hard, which he probably did. 'Is all this important?'

'I'm always interested in the hired help.' I could have added that I was interested in finding out why Marvin had wanted to kill me, but I didn't say so. 'Now, you mentioned your wife. What about her?'

'She has disappeared. She left home two days ago, hasn't been seen or heard from since. I'm worried, Lantry.'

'A natural emotion. Have you been to the police?'

'No.'

'Why not? They are the most suitable and obvious people to find her. They can check the hospitals, the morgue, the—'

'I have already done that,' he interrupted impatiently. 'I am not wholly a fool, Lantry. When Norma, my wife, didn't return home, I had my lawyers check every possible place she might be.' He looked baffled. 'They couldn't find her.'

'And you think I could?'

'Yes. I think that if any man could find her, you are that man.'

'Thank you.' It was a compliment and it was sincere. I poised my pencil. 'I take it that your wife is an elderly woman?'

'No.' He licked his thin lips with a nervous gesture, a quick, darting movement of his tongue. 'This is my second marriage,' he explained. 'My first wife died a short while ago and I married again.'

'I see. Children?'

'Two. My son, Stephan, is twenty-five. My daughter, Susan, is a year younger. There are no children of my second marriage.' He didn't say that there wouldn't be, but it was as plain as the nose on his face.

'They live with you?'

'Yes. They live with Norma and I. We have a few servants and do little entertaining.' He coughed and took a square of linen from his pocket. 'Is all this essential, Lantry?'

'It could be.' I waited until he had finished dabbing at his lips. 'About your second wife, Colonel?'

'I married her about six months ago. She was, is, a sweet child, rather headstrong, but that is to be expected.' He didn't seem to have noticed his slip. 'Our relationship was more that of father and daughter than husband and wife.'

I nodded, not believing him, but I wasn't paid to give opinions. 'History?'

'What?' He blinked. 'Is that necessary?'

'You want me to find her, don't you?' I leaned back in my chair. 'What am I supposed to do, go round asking every woman I meet whether or not she is your missing wife?' I shrugged. 'At thirty dollars a day plus expenses, I'd be willing to spend the rest of my life on the job. Can you afford to wait that long?'

'I have a photograph here.' He slipped an oblong of pasteboard from an inner pocket. 'You will find all relevant details on the back.'

'Good.' I didn't touch the photograph. 'Now, who saw her last? Who spoke to her last? Where did she say she was going? Has she any friends? Did she take her car? Clothes? Money?' I shrugged at his expression.

'I'm sorry, Colonel, but I'm not a miracle worker. I'll find your wife, but I must have something to work on.'

'She has a car, but didn't take it with her. As for clothes?' He made a helpless gesture. 'I don't know about that. She has a lot of clothes and, frankly, I wouldn't know if she took any or not.'

'She has a maid?'

'Naturally.'

'Good.' I made more pothooks. 'I'll call and see her tomorrow. Which address? Town or Lower Manhattan?'

'Manhattan. 518 Osbourne Heights, but is it necessary for you to visit my house?'

'It would be simpler.' I jotted down the address and picked up the photograph. Despite myself it was hard to keep a blank expression. Something of what I felt must have showed in my face.

'I am an old man,' the Colonel said quietly. 'I married first rather late in life and am forty years older than my children.' He looked at me. 'I am a rich man also, and a rich man can sometimes indulge his whims. I wanted a young wife and, perhaps not surprisingly, my wealth outweighed her desire for a younger man.'

'I see.' I laid the photograph face down on the desk. 'You are a cynic, Colonel.'

'Not a cynic,' he corrected. 'An intelligent man.' He reached into an inside pocket and produced a wallet. From it he counted out five nice, crisp, one-hundred-dollar bills. He laid them on the desk. 'I do not wish to haggle,' he said, and I felt an instinctive warmth towards him. 'You mentioned thirty dollars a day plus

expenses, expenses which, I imagine, would be some-
what high.'

'Gas, drinks, bullets, and bribes,' I said quickly. He
didn't seem to have heard me.

'I will make my own offer. Here is five hundred
dollars. Take it, and the day you find my wife I will give
you ten thousand more.' He pushed the bills towards
me, their newness making little crackling noises. 'You
accept?'

'I accept.' I reached into the drawer, the one I keep
my bottle and spare gun in, and took out a pad of
receipts. I filled in the top form, signed it, and handed
it over. Geeson took it, examined it, then tucked it into
his wallet.

'Is that all?'

'Not quite.' I stared down at the pothooks I'd made
to refresh my memory. 'I should like to interview your
son and daughter. Would tomorrow be a convenient
time? I could check with the maid at the same time.'

'You forget yourself, Lantry,' he said coldly. 'You
may interview the servants, yes. But my personal
family must not be bothered by you. After all, even at
best you are little more than a paid servant yourself.'

'Is that what you think?' I picked up the bills and
knocked their edges flush on the scarred surface of the
desk. 'Here.' I held them out to him. 'Take them, return
my receipt, and then get out of here.'

'What!' He was more than startled, he was shocked.
'I don't understand.'

'You've picked the wrong man,' I said tightly. 'If you

want a yes-sirring lap-dog you won't find him here. Good night, Colonel. Don't trip over the body.'

He flushed, his wrinkled skin warming to the unusual flow of blood, and his hands, as he gripped his cane, showed tense the knuckles white with strain. I thought that he was going to hit me, and I didn't care if he tried. He swallowed.

'Could you recommend such a man?'

'A dozen,' I said cheerfully. 'They will take your money and dance to your tune. They will wipe their feet and remember to say "sir," and they'll be very, very polite. But they won't find your wife and, if they do find anything else, they'll make you pay for it—but good.'

'Blackmail?'

'I didn't say that.'

'But you meant it.'

I shrugged and pointed to a certificate hanging on the wall. 'You see that? It's a licence, issued by the county authorities, and it says that I'm duly qualified to operate as a private detective. Those licences don't grow on trees, Colonel, and you don't get them by sending in box tops. Your money will buy you more than me just doing as I'm told, but you just don't own enough to buy my soul.'

'Arrogance,' he whispered, and sat staring down at the floor. He must have been desperate, because he didn't get up and walk out. Instead he looked at me. 'What do you want?'

'If I take the case, I'll do what has to be done, but I'll

do it in my own way. I won't interfere with you and I won't make myself more of a nuisance than I can help, but I want access to your home, to your servants, and to your children.' I picked up the money. 'Is it a deal?'

'On one condition.' He hesitated and I knew what was coming. I tried to help him out.

'I cannot condone law-breaking,' I warned. 'I can't cover up murder or—'

'Murder!' He was startled this time, not shocked. Startled and a little scared. 'Who said anything about murder?'

'An example.' I dismissed the notion with a wave of my hand. The movement made me remember the cigarette I was still holding, so I dropped it. 'However, that doesn't mean I act as a policeman, I won't. I won't pry and I won't squeal. Does that answer you?'

'Perhaps.' He stared at me from hooded eyes. 'If you find my wife. Lantry, I want you to let me know first. *First*, understand?'

'Yes.'

'Agreed then.' He nodded, a sharp inclination of his head, and rose to his feet. 'Tomorrow, then?'

'Tomorrow.'

I led the way out of the office.

The tough chauffeur had gone. Probably he was nursing his swollen jaw and injured pride downstairs by the car. His gun had gone too, and I hoped that he wouldn't try to kill anyone with it before he bought more bullets. I signalled for the elevator and stood, trying not to shiver, as it groaned its slow way up from the basement. Geeson stared distastefully down the dark corridor, leaning heavily on his cane, and I felt sorry for him.

It must have been terrible for a man with all his money to have to come out on a cold, wet night. It must have been a shame for him to have hired a private eye to do what the police could have done for nothing. It must have been ever more terrible that a young and virile woman should have decided that money couldn't compensate for old bones and thin blood.

The elevator groaned to a stop, and the old man who was spending the last few years of his life jerked open the doors. He scowled at me—I probably woke him up—then slammed the cage as the Colonel stepped inside.

I shrugged and stepped back into the office.

I had five hundred dollars for a case which, on the face of it, was no case, and the prospect of ten thousand more to come. I should have felt good. I should have felt wonderful, but I didn't, and even when I took a drink the whisky burned my throat instead of warming my stomach.

I dropped the empty bottle and stepped across to the window. Outside it was still raining, the neon signs kept flashing and, far below, the black limousine still waited like a big black beetle against the kerb. A figure crossed to it, an old man leaning on a cane, and a second figure limped towards it and opened the rear door.

With a white plume trailing from the exhaust, the

big car slid down the rain-swept street and I watched it go, half envious of its obvious comfort and class. A shadow moved in a doorway opposite, a dim, shapeless blob with a pale splotch for a face and two more for hands. It stared up at me before hunching itself along the street, head down against the rain.

I shivered.

It was a hell of a night.

CHAPTER THREE

The next day dawned cloudy but dry. I hurried through my toilet, trying not to feel the cold and knowing that winter would soon be coating the streets with ice and slush. I shaved carefully over the scar and took trouble with my hair. I chose the double-breasted, grey worsted suit, one I'd had made when I'd been able to afford a really good cloth. It had a fine stripe and a faint check, and the tailor had known what he was doing. With the suit I chose black Oxfords, a white shirt, and decided on a ten-dollar, hand-painted tie I'd given myself for a birthday present and only worn once.

I tucked a silk handkerchief in my breast pocket and settled the shoulder holster more comfortably beneath my arm. From the bedside table I picked up my gun, checked the loading, then slipped the 9mm Browning into its resting place. I like the Browning and I like the calibre. Some men go in for a .45 Service automatic, others like a Luger, and one man I knew used to favour an Italian Berreta until it jammed one day when he needed it and he collected a dozen slugs. Still, each man to his choice, and I'd found that the fifteen-shot magazine gave me an edge over the boys who liked to count shots.

It also saved me carrying an extra clip.

I smoothed my jacket, the cut of the suit hiding the bulge of the gun, and slipped into my gabardine raincoat. A soft, matching grey, snap-brimmed fedora, and I was ready for breakfast.

I was also ready to visit ten million dollars.

Over a stack of wheatcakes drenched in maple syrup, I gave some thought to my midnight visitors. It wasn't their arrival at midnight which made me think; there's more business done between dusk and dawn than most citizens know about. No, it was why the Colonel should call on me at all. I was still thinking about it when Pug dropped into the seat opposite to me and looked hopefully at my empty plate.

'Hello, Mike,' he said forlornly. 'Anything doing?'

I stared at him, looking at the obvious signs of a recent battering, and beneath my stare he flushed.

'You've been in the ring again,' I accused. 'So much for promises.'

'Aw, Mike,' He squirmed as though he was a small boy instead of a two-hundred-and-twenty-pound bruiser. 'Looie offered me ten bucks, win, lose, or draw, and I was hungry.'

That was an understatement. Pug Berson was always hungry, had always been hungry ever since he could remember. He had tried to fight his way out of the slums with his fists and fallen in with a bunch of bright boys who had thrown him to the wolves. Almost punch-drunk, desperate, ready for anything, he had been easy meat for a gambling ring who believed in making sure of winning before the bout ever started.

Pug was honest, as honest as any man could be who had come up the hard way, and he'd refused to take a fall. So, just to show him, they gave him a nice, easy, one-way ticket to the electric chair by means of a gang killing, and enough circumstantial evidence to fry a saint. A frame-up, sure, but who was to worry?

I did. I'd found the killer and sprung Pug, and he'd never forgotten it.

He never let me forget it either.

'Okay, so you were hungry.' I snapped my fingers at the waitress and she came gliding over. 'Repeat order, doubled, and two cups of coffee.' I waited until she'd brought Pug his breakfast, lit a cigarette, and while waiting for my coffee to cool, examined the photograph the Colonel had left with me.

It was a colour print, a good job, and could even be a good likeness, if you made allowance for the touching up. The data on the back read: height, 5 ft. 5 ins.; bust, 34; hips 35; weight, 95 lbs.; waist, 25; colour, blonde; complexion, fair; scars, none; other distinguishing marks, none; age, twenty-eight.

All of which made her just one of maybe twenty million women.

The face was something else. I discounted fifty per cent of what I saw, and what remained still made her something special. I could see why Geeson wanted her back.

The waitress came over and began to sweep away a

few non-existent crumbs. I reached for my wallet and took out one of the brand-new bills. Her eyes almost slid from their sockets as I laid it in front of her.

'Gee!' She stared at the bill as if she'd never seen one like it before, which she probably hadn't. 'Haven't you got anything smaller?'

'No, crack it for me, will you?' I stared again at the colour print, memorising it, studying the bone structure, ears, eyes, hair-line, the shape of the mouth. Faces can be disguised, but some things can never be hidden. By the time the waitress returned with my change, I could have picked out the missing woman from a crowd scene in a movie.

Pug gulped the last of his coffee and reached for the photograph.

'Anyone I know?'

'Maybe.' I passed him the print. 'Take a look.'

He did, a long one, then whistled.

'Some dame, eh! Yours?'

'Colonel Geeson's. His wife. He wants her back.'

'A powder.' He nodded, with the wisdom of the slums. 'Fell for some rich guy.'

'The Colonel,' I explained, 'has ten million dollars. Try again.'

'What's the use? A dame, no kind of dame, ever runs from that kind of dough. You got to find her?'

'That's the general idea.' I could talk to Pug and, sometimes, he managed to put his finger on the one thing so obvious no one would see it. 'Try it for size, Pug. You're a woman, good-looking, young, married to a rich guy who is liable to kick the bucket any moment. What would make you run away?'

He thought about it, screwing his eyes and rubbing the scarred knuckles of his hands. Watching him think almost made me feel tired, it was such hard work.

'Forget it,' I said wearily. 'It's no easier for you than for me.' I reached out to pick up the print where it was lying on the table between us.

'Hold it!' Pug rested one big paw on the photograph. 'I've seen this dame before.' He frowned with the effort required to think. 'At the fights. She used to run around with Thornedyke's mob.'

'You're crazy!' I snatched up the print and put it in my pocket. 'What would a woman like her be doing with that heel?'

'Why ask me?' Pug looked baffled. 'I'm sure I've seen her with him. Let me see,' he stared up at the fly-blown ceiling. 'Two years ago? Three? Hell, how can I remember?'

'After that beating you took last night, you can't.' I got up from the table and he trotted after me as I headed for the door.

'Say, Mike!' He stood before me and I guessed what was coming. Not a touch, Pug wasn't a bum, but he had a pathetic belief that I needed him to protect me. Sometimes I did. Sometimes his weight and brawn had saved me from a nasty beating, but I couldn't see the Colonel's servants ganging up on me with lead pipes and razors. I had an idea.

'Listen.' I took out the print and shoved it into his

hand. I took out some money, ten dollars, and put it with the photograph. 'Make the rounds. Check the hospitals and accident wards. Drop in at the morgue and ask around in the dives. She may have been taken in without identity. She may even be suffering from amnesia or something. Get around and cover the field. If she's in trouble she may not want publicity. Find her, Pug, and I'll cut you in a C note.'

'A hundred bucks.' He beamed with gratitude. 'Sure, Mike, I'll do it.' He hesitated. 'You certain that you don't want me with you, just in case?'

'Not this trip.' I shoved him towards the kerb. 'On your way, sleuth, and don't report back until you find something.'

I watched as his big figure dwindled and lost itself in the crowd. A waste of time? Sure, but he'd come to no harm making the double-check and, for all I knew, he could strike it lucky. He wouldn't be looking for Mrs. Geeson, of course, I knew him well enough for that. She would be his sister, his wife, his girlfriend, anything he could think of to legitimise his questions. He might even find her. Might. I doubted it.

But it got him out of my hair.

Glancing at my wristwatch, I saw that the banks would be open by now. I walked half a mile and deposited three of the bills at my bank, grinning as I imagined how the manager would be now that he could meet certain cheques without having to decide between bouncing them back or giving me an overdraft.

From the bank I caught the elevated to Osbourne

Heights, changing to a cab in order to ride the couple of miles to my destination. I could have taken a streetcar, but didn't. I'm not a snob, but I had to keep up a front, and it was lucky I did. The drive must have been all of a mile long. Paying off the cab, I pressed the door-bell and, while I waited, glanced at the weather-stained front of the big, brownstone house and the trimmed lawn before it. I was busy wondering what a convu-lated piece of moss-covered stone was supposed to represent when the door opened and a discreet cough warned me that I was not alone.

I handed the butler my card. 'The Colonel probably left orders about me,' I said. 'Is he at home?'

'No, sir.' The butler glanced at the card in his hand. I'd given him one of my personal cards, the one which doesn't say anything about my business, but I could see that he wasn't impressed. 'The Colonel did mention you, Mr. Lantry. I understand that you wish to question Marie.'

'Marie?' I stepped into a hall which could have been hired out as a taxi-dancers' step-around, and the door swung shut with a click from its patent lock.

'Madam's maid,' explained the butler. 'I will send for her at once.'

'Just a minute—er?'

'Harmond, sir.'

'You know my name already, Harmond.' I grinned at him, and some of the ice thawed from his weak old eyes. 'Are the children at home?'

'I believe so, sir. Shall I inform them of your presence?'

'Later.' I stared at him, trying to read beyond the professional mask. Servants aren't as dumb as most people like to think, and I'd have wagered half of what I owned that Harmond knew more of what went on in the house than the owner did. If he wanted to he could be a great help.

'You know why I'm here, Harmond?'

'No, sir,' he lied.

'But you could guess.' I handed him one of my professional cards. He glanced at it and somehow, in some subtle way, his face altered.

'Madam?'

'Yes.'

'I see. Are you connected with the official police?'

'No.' I stared at him. 'I want to find her, Harmond. Do you want me to?'

'Indeed, yes, sir.' He seemed about to say more, then his face froze back into its original mask. 'I will inform Marie that you are waiting, sir. If you will remain in the library I will send her to you.'

I followed him into a small, book-lined room, where he left me alone with the mouldering volumes. Marie came in just as I was wondering whether it would be best to start reading a book or to go in search of her. As soon as I saw her, I could tell that she knew what I was and what I wanted.

She was small, pretty in a hard, cynical way, and if it hadn't been for her powder and phony French accent she would have been quite attractive. I smiled at her and offered her a cigarette.

'Did the Colonel tell you to expect me, Marie?'

'*Oui, monsieur.*'

'*C'est bon Alors*, did *moi*—'

'Okay, wise guy,' she said wearily. 'So I'm not French. What do you want to know?'

'What clothes, if any, did the Colonel's wife take with her when she left?'

'None.'

'None?' I raised my eyebrows. 'In this weather? She must have been pretty hot-blooded to walk naked in early winter.'

'Joke,' she said flatly. 'Ha, ha, ha.'

'Then what did she take?'

'What she was wearing.'

'So?'

'Well, the usual underthings.' She darted a vicious glance at me. 'Want me to elaborate?'

'I can guess. What else?'

'A brown tweed costume. A chartreuse blouse, green shoes, nylons, fur coat, hat, purse, and gloves.' She rattled off the list as though she had learned it by heart. I looked up from my notebook.

'What kind of fur coat?'

'Silver fox, three-quarter length.'

'What colour hat and gloves?'

'Black, I think.'

'Don't think, be sure. What colour?'

'Black.' This time she was certain, and I knew that I wouldn't get a different answer no matter how hard I tried. 'Jewellery?'

'A stack of it. Wristwatch, gold and studded with diamonds. Two bracelets, one of rubies and diamonds, the other emeralds. Four sets of earrings, a couple of ropes of pearls, some dress clips, and a hatful of rings.'

'A lot of jewellery.'

'Most of what she had.' Marie sounded vicious, and I wondered why. 'She cleaned out the jewellery box but good. Now, I suppose, some gumshoe will accuse me of helping myself.'

'Why should they?'

'I know coppers.' Marie dragged at her cigarette. 'Anything else?'

'Did she take any suitcases?'

'No.'

'Then she must have shoved the jewellery in her pockets or purse?'

'I guess she must have done.' Marie shrugged. 'She was always a crazy dame; I guess she just got fed up with the old man and took a powder with all the portable loot.'

'What make you say that? Did they fight?'

'Not so's you'd notice,' she admitted. 'But she was always chasing off and leaving him to worry about her. If you ask me, he began to regret having married a tramp.'

'She was in the habit of taking off, was she?' I crushed out my cigarette and slipped the notebook back into my pocket. 'Any idea where she went to?'

'No.'

'Did she ever talk to you about her friends?'

'No.'

'Not much help, are you, Marie?'

'No.'

'I see.' I took out another cigarette and poised it in front of my mouth. 'Why do you think she's dead, Marie?'

'Dead!' Now she looked scared for the first time. 'I didn't say that.'

'Yes, you did. Not right out, maybe, but in other ways. Why else would you be afraid of someone thinking that maybe you've helped yourself to the jewellery? If she was still alive, the question would never arise.' I dropped the cigarette and gripped her shoulders. 'Come on, Marie, give! What do you know?'

'Nothing!' She wriggled and I held on. 'I don't know nothing, I tell you.'

'Is she dead?'

'I don't know!' She was getting frantic by now. 'Honest to God, shamus, I don't know!'

I believed her. I let her go and she rubbed the places where my fingers had dug. Her eyes told me she hated me, but they told me more than that. Marie was scared, plenty scared, and I wondered why.

I was still wondering when she ran out of the room and slammed the door behind her.

CHAPTER FOUR

Harmond must have been waiting outside, because when I opened the door he was standing at my side.

'Mr. Lantry, sir.'

'Yes?'

'If I could have a private word with you, sir?'

'Sure.' I turned back towards the library, but he stepped back and looked uncomfortable.

'Not here, sir. Later perhaps? At your office?'

'Why not? You have my card. Give me a ring or, better still, make it for tonight. Can do?'

'Ten o'clock, sir?'

'That'll do fine.' I grinned at him, knowing better than to try and force his confidence. He would talk when he was ready to talk and not a moment before. I changed the subject. 'Is the boy home? Mr. Stephan, I mean?'

'You want to see him, sir?' Harmond looked troubled.

'Yes. I—' I broke off, staring at a man who had just appeared from the rear of the building.

He was young, tall, with a mottled face and a weak chin. His eyes matched his chin and his clothes looked as though they'd been slept in. He reeked of stale smoke and stale liquor. He held an empty bottle in one hand.

'Harmond! Damn you, man! Where have you been?'

'Here, sir.' The butler didn't seem to touch the floor as he glided towards the young man. 'Yes, Mr Stephan?'

'Bring me a bottle. Bring me two bottles. Bring me the whole damn cellar.' Stephan swayed and almost fell. His bleared eyes focused and he blinked at me, grinning in a foolish, empty way, and waving his empty bottle. 'Hi, stranger! You wanna drink?'

I didn't answer and it seemed to annoy him.

'You there! Who the hell are you, anyway?'

'This is Mr. Lantry, sir,' said Harmond. 'Your father asked him to call.'

'What about?'

'Maybe I could answer that.' I stepped forward and smiled at the drink. 'How about letting me join you in a snort?'

He thought about it. He let the idea soak into his mind, and I could almost see the wheels go round as he pushed away the alcohol fog to make room for a new idea. He nodded.

'Sure, why not?'

I looked at Harmond, who vanished to get more supplies, then followed my host into a room.

Once it had been a study, but now the only studying done in it was of the relative merits of different brands of liquor. Some paintings hung on the walls, and I thought of Reubens and Titian and other Renaissance painters. There were some books, a desk, and something which could have been a filing cabinet. There was a typewriter standing in the middle of a mass of crumpled paper, and a tape-recorder had been knocked to the floor.

But the main item of study was shown by the bottles which littered the room.

Harmond knocked and I relieved him of a tray bearing a fifth of rye, a syphon, and a couple of clean glasses. I was glad of the clean glasses. I opened the bottle and sniffed at the contents. I'm not too fond of rye, myself. If I'm going to drink hard liquor I like Scotch. I'd settle for cognac if I can't get Scotch, but mostly I have to drink what's around.

This was one of those times.

I tilted the bottle over the glass, poured out a generous three fingers into each, and passed one to Stephan. I raised the other in a toast.

'To us.'

'To crime,' he corrected, and downed his drink at a gulp. I refilled his glass.

'To crime,' he said again, and swallowed the dose as before. I was curious.

'Why do you say that?'

'Say what?'

'To crime.' I motioned with my glass. 'What's so good about it to drink to?'

'Why not?' He leaned forward, a strange expression in his bloodshot eyes, and a lock of hair fell over his forehead, giving him a peculiarly boyish look. If you can imagine a boy with the bloated face of a drunkard and a glass of liquor in his hand.

'Listen, my friend.' He wagged a finger at me. 'In a world in which everyone has been pressed down to a neutral grey, your criminal is your modern adventurer. He flies in the face of authority, and with the skill of his body and brain, cuts a path for himself and so makes his own destiny.' He dribbled rye down his chin. 'You agree?'

'Sure,' I said dryly. 'Most of our so-called criminals are victims of society. They never had a chance and, by hitting against the law, they assert their independence.' I forgot where I had originally heard that patter—from some long-haired social worker, probably, but whoever it was had obviously never been mugged and rolled, never had his home broken into or felt the burning kiss of a razor as it slashed his cheek.

If he had, then he'd never have uttered such rubbish.

Stephan nodded, pleased with me for agreeing with him.

'Good,' he said unsteadily. 'Tell me more.'

'You tell me.' I sipped my drink and, setting it down, lit a cigarette. 'I'm interested in your mother. I—'

'My *what*!' He jerked to his feet, and the glass fell from his hand, bouncing and rolling until it came to rest against the leg of a table. I picked it up.

'Your father's wife,' I explained. 'His first one. Your mother.'

'Oh.' He licked his lips and stared at me in a kind of glassy semi-stupor. 'I thought that you meant—' He shook his head. 'Never mind that now. What do you know?'

'When did she die?'

'My mother? About two years ago. Why?'

'Nothing, just asking.' I dragged at my cigarette. 'Was she a fit woman? Did she enjoy good health?'

'She died in a car accident,' he said tightly, and something of the private hell in which he lived peered out through his bleared eyes. I poured rye into his glass and handed it to him.

'So she died in a car accident.' I nodded. 'And your step-mother? When did your father first meet her?'

'Norma? About nine months after the accident. I wouldn't know.'

'Not know?' I put just the right amount of incredulity into my voice, and it acted as the spur I hoped it would.

'Yes,' he snarled. 'I know. I know just when he did meet her, damn him!'

'So you knew her first?' It was a guess, but I hit the target.

'I did. We ran around together. It was fun while it lasted, but it didn't last. Mother died and the Colonel saw Norma. He saw her and took her, just like that.' He tried to snap his fingers, but couldn't make it. 'He bought her, paid for her with my mother's money. Ninety-five pounds of warm, living flesh. At how much the pound?' He giggled. 'You ask him. I did, and he almost threw me out, he and that damned chauffeur of his, and she stood there and laughed at me when they did it. Laughed, and laughed and—'

He swayed, the glass falling from his hand, then, as if all the life had gone out of him, he toppled and fell towards the floor.

I caught him as he fell.

I held him for a moment before letting him settle gently on the floor. I searched for a button to summon help, but couldn't find one. So I opened the door, and there, as I'd expected, stood Harmond.

'Stephan.' I jerked my head backwards into the room. 'He's passed out.'

'I understand, sir.' The old butler swallowed, and if I hadn't been there he would have wiped his eyes. 'The poor devil,' he murmured. 'The poor, poor, devil.'

'Need any help?'

'No thank you, sir.'

'You've known him a long time, Harmond. How long has he been like this?'

'Only since just after his mother died, sir.'

'Since the Colonel married his girlfriend?'

'I wouldn't know, Mr. Lantry.' He did know, but he wasn't telling. He stepped past me and picked up the youth as though he had been a baby. I stepped in front of him and stared into his eyes.

'Ten o'clock, Harmond.'

'Yes, sir. I will be there.'

I let him go then and poured myself another drink. It was good liquor, even though it was the wrong kind for my taste, so I savoured it, rolling it around my tongue and tried to appreciate the burnt, wood-smoke flavour. I wandered around the room and stared at one of the paintings. It intrigued me; I couldn't tell in this light whether it was genuine or not, but if it was it was worth a lot of money. When I turned round again, a girl stood in the doorway watching me with a peculiar, half-contemptuous, half-timid stare.

'Well?'

'Well what?'

'You wanted to see me, didn't you?' She advanced towards me, a cigarette held casually in her red-tipped fingers, her dress clinging to her youthful, lissome figure. She stopped beside me, the top of her head coming about level with the lobe of my ear. That made her about five feet eight inches tall, say five-five if you discounted her high heels. I had already guessed her weight.

'You're Susan,' I said. 'Stephan's sister.'

'I'm Susan,' she admitted. 'And you're the big, tough, private eye whose going to find my dear stepmother.' She looked around the room. 'Where is Stephan, by the way?'

'Asleep.'

'Drunk, you mean.' She sniffed the air and glanced distastefully at the empty bottles littering the floor. 'He's always drunk.'

'Maybe he has a reason.' I gestured towards the typewriter. 'His?'

'Yes.' She explained without being asked. 'He's trying to write a play. He's been trying for a long time now and he's still working on the first act.'

'I bet that I could guess the plot,' I said. She shrugged.

'No prize. Well, what can I do for you?'

I didn't answer straight away, but spent some time looking at her. Young, supple, and yet beneath her makeup she showed signs of strain. A brittle tiredness, as if she just couldn't bother to care any longer, and a recklessness which didn't match the softness of her lips and eyes.

'I'm trying to find your step-mother,' I said. 'I can do it either of two ways, the hard way or the easy. If you want to help, it needn't turn out to be so hard. Will you help me?'

'How?'

'Tell me what you know about her, who her friends are, where she might be, the usual thing.'

'Isn't that what you're supposed to do?' She crossed towards the bottle and poured herself a drink. 'I don't know Norma any too well. She isn't much older than I am, and I suppose I resented her coming to live here. We don't get along too well.'

'Your fault or hers?'

'Mine, probably.' Susan shrugged. 'I'm afraid that I can't help you, Mr. Lantry. All I know is that she didn't turn up one morning at breakfast.'

'Mike,' I said.

'Mike?'

'My name, we can dispense with the "mister".' I joined her in a drink. 'Here's to crime.'

'Good old crime,' she said dully. 'For you, money in the bank. For us and people like us, trouble, lots of it.' She bit her lips and for a moment I thought that she was going to cry 'To hell with crime!'

'A sensible woman.' I put down my untasted drink and looked at her. 'At least, you don't think that she's dead.'

'Norma? Why should she be?'

'Just an idea I had.'

'It's possible,' she agreed. 'But if anything had happened to her, we'd know, wouldn't we? I mean, an accident or anything like that.'

'I wasn't thinking of accident,' I said deliberately.

'Murder! Ridiculous!'

'Or suicide?'

'Don't be stupid.' She was really upset now. 'I'm not too fond of Norma, but she wouldn't do a thing like that. Why should she?'

'Why ask me? I only work here.' I picked up my drink again and swallowed it. 'You saw her every day; did she seem upset, worried, something like that?'

'Not that I noticed.'

'Your brother is in love with her, isn't he?'

'Is he?'

'Is your father in love with her?'

'Why don't you ask him.' She moved away from me and I could see that now she was really angry. 'I suggest, Mr. Lantry, that you concentrate on the job, and forget about prying into things which can't possibly concern you.'

'Sorry,' I said. 'Just one more question. When she didn't turn up for breakfast, questions must have been asked. I'd like you to tell me if anyone saw her leave the house during the night.'

'Why don't you ask the staff?'

'I'm asking you because I want the correct answer. By now the staff know that something is wrong and they won't be eager to say anything to incriminate themselves. I'm not a cop, but I'm the nearest thing to one, and most people are shy of the law. Well?'

'No one saw her,' she said after a moment. 'No one at all.'

'Thank you.' I nodded as though she had done me a favour and moved towards the door. 'Sorry to have troubled you.'

She didn't answer, and I had the impression she was glad to see me go.

Harmond let me out, his face expressionless, and I stood for a moment staring at the lawn. The gravelled drive swung in a wide loop before the house, joining up with itself on the other side of the moss-grown statue and running between a tall avenue of trees. An extension of the drive led around the house towards the garage, and I followed it, my Oxfords crunching on the clean stones.

I found Marvin hard at work polishing the big limousine. He glanced at me, thinned his lips, and went on polishing.

I waited for about two minutes standing wide-legged, my hands thrust into the pockets of my gabardine, not speaking, not moving, not doing anything but stare at the busy man. At the end of that time his nerve broke and he dropped his duster.

'What the hell do you want?'

I stared at him. A good-looking young man with thick curly hair, nice nose, and healthy cheeks. His eyes were anxious.

'How's the leg?'

'What's that to you?' He stepped forward, not too far, but far enough so that I could see the limp had vanished. I shook my head.

'You've got the wrong idea. I've come to give you something, not argue about what happened.' I took one of my hands from my pocket and held out a ten-dollar bill. 'Here, buy yourself some more cartridges for that mail-order gun of yours.'

He said a bad word.

'Then buy some linament for that jaw.' I dropped the bill on to the gravel, and automatically his eyes followed it. When he looked up again, I was inside the garage.

It held three cars. The limousine, an estate car, and a small convertible. It could have held more, but the vacant space was littered with tools and tyres, cans of oil, and a portable air-generator. I leaned casually over the side of the convertible.

'Which is Mrs. Geeson's car?'

'You're leaning on it.'

'I see. You and the other servants use the estate car, and the Colonel the limousine. What do the children use?'

'They don't own cars.'

'How come?'

'When the Colonel's first wife died in that car crash, the Colonel sold them. He said that one accident in a family was one too many, and he didn't want any more. If they want to go anywhere, I drive them.'

'And if you're not here?'

'They phone for a private car. We've an account with the Blue Star Company. They provide a car and driver at any time.'

I nodded and sat down on the edge of a bench. I looked for a cigarette and found only an empty packet. I was looking at it when the chauffeur offered me one of his own.

'Thanks.' I snapped my lighter and offered him a light in return. We both inhaled and stared at each other.

'How long have you worked for the Colonel, Peter?'

'Three years.'

'So you were here when the old lady died?'

'Yes.'

'How did it happen?'

'Burst front tyre. She wasn't all that old and still liked to drive herself.' He looked at me. 'Why all the questions? I thought that you'd been hired to find Norma.'

'Norma?'

'We all call her that.' He seemed uncomfortable. 'Hell, she isn't any older than I am.'

'That's right. Are you carrying a torch for her too?'

'Me?' He seemed to be surprised. 'What gave you that idea?'

I shrugged. 'It's been known to happen before.

You're young, good-looking, and always around. The Colonel is old, but he has the money. A smart woman could figure a way to combine the two.'

This time he almost got me. If I hadn't been watching for it I'd never have known what hit me, but I saw him move, and by the time he swung I was well out of the way. I pushed and he grunted as he slammed against the edge of the bench. He turned, a wrench in his hand, and came towards me.

'You dirty shamus,' he gritted. 'I'm going to open that skull of yours and let the fresh air clean up what's inside. I—' He stopped, looking at the Browning in my hand.

'Put down that wrench,' I said quietly. 'That's better. So I made a mistake. But I've been hired to do a job and I'm going to do it. You can help me or get in my way, I don't care what you do, but the next time we play, we play for keeps.' I dropped the cigarette and trod it to ruins against the concrete floor of the garage. I hefted the gun and put it away. I didn't need it, hadn't needed it, but I was in no mood for trading punches. Marvin hesitated.

'You're wasting your time,' he said. 'Norma took a powder and run out on the old man. So what?'

'So I'm going to find her. Any ideas?'

'No, and if I had any, I wouldn't tell you.'

'Look, Marvin,' I said patiently. 'Twice now you've tried to beat me up for no apparent reason. You're not a hood or a bum, you wouldn't just do a thing like that for the laughs, so there must be something you know and I don't.' I stared at him. 'You don't want me to find her, do you.' The way I said it didn't make it a question.

He didn't answer.

'Okay, so you don't want to tell me. Tell me this, then. Did you drive Norma into town the night she vanished?'

'No.'

'How about that company, the Blue Star?'

'We phoned them,' he said sullenly. 'No dice.'

'Then she must have walked.'

'Or phoned for a cab,' he suggested. 'She could have done that.'

'Without anyone seeing her leave?'

'Why not?' He shifted uncomfortably. 'Why ask me, anyway? I'm only the chauffeur around here.'

'It might be a good idea,' I said pointedly, 'if you remembered that.'

I left him then, staring after me and hating me with his eyes. I didn't let it worry me. I've been looked at that way before and I'm still warm and moving around, but the people who did the looking, quite a few of them anyway, are cold and very, very still.

The wind had risen a little as I started the long walk down the drive and powdery flakes of snow tried to push their way between my neck and collar, I pulled it higher around my ears, gave the brim of my hat a downward tug, and stepped out a little faster.

I should have asked Marvin for a lift.

CHAPTER FIVE

By the time I got back to Times Square, both my watch and my stomach told me that it was time to eat. I turned into a restaurant and ordered a thick steak, medium rare, with all the trimmings. While waiting for it I picked up a discarded newspaper. One item caught my eye, and I read it again.

> 'What daughter of what Army man (retired) has been chasing the black and red too long and too heavily for her own good? There's danger in them there colours, gal. Watch it.'

It didn't need much imagination to guess that Susan had been chancing the family wealth on the illegal gambling tables run by some of New York's more prosperous citizens.

The food arrived then and I shelved the problem while I fed the inner man. After coffee I paid the bill, bought a couple of packets of cigarettes, then made my way down to the towering building of the *New York Tribune*. The prim, buck-toothed woman in charge of the reference section greeted me with a glare, and I tried to thaw her frigid soul with a warm smile.

'Good afternoon, madam.' I showed her one of my cards. 'Could you help me? I'd like access to the morgue.'

The morgue was the place where they kept all the information ever collected on every person who had ever been in print. Normally it was closed to the public, but I had hopes of getting inside and saving some time. She had other ideas.

'You may use the reference section,' she said coldly. 'You can read the back issues, but the morgue is reserved for newspaper men only.'

'This is a special case,' I said hopefully. 'I'm working on something urgent and I could waste days trying to find what I need. If you'd help me I could be out of here in an hour.'

I paused, staring at her and switching on the charm. It didn't work.

'The reference section is to your right,' she said coldly, and bent her head over her desk. I felt like shaking her, but I knew that it wouldn't be any good. I was standing there wondering whether or not to try a bribe when someone called to me.

'Mike! How goes it?'

I turned and grinned with relief and admiration at the trim figure coming towards me. I liked Constance Young. I'd liked her ever since I first met her in a downtown bar when she'd been a cub reporter trying to crack down a case. I'd saved her from a nasty experience and we'd kept more or less in touch ever since. I grabbed her arm and told her what the trouble was.

She sniffed.

'Why didn't you ask for me, Mike? I can get you in.' She smiled at the prim woman and led the way past the barrier. I smiled too, but the prim woman didn't smile. She stared after us with a mouth which reminded me of a lemon, it was that sour.

Inside the morgue I told. Constance what the trouble was.

'Norma Geeson?' She nodded. 'The Colonel's second wife. There should be some coverage here. The wedding, the accident, things like that.'

'Find them for me, will you, sweet?' I gave her a cigarette and we blew smoke against the 'No Smoking' sign. She stared at me.

'A story?'

'Could be.'

'Come off it, Mike. You wouldn't be interested in the files unless you hoped to dig up some dirt. I want in.'

She did too. Young as she was, Constance was still the eager-eyed reporter hot on the scent of a scoop. I smiled at her and shook my head.

'I can't tell you, Constance. Professional ethics, but this I will promise, if I get anything for publication, it's yours. Fair enough?'

'I suppose so.' She yelled at a small man wearing a green eyeshield and dirty suspenders. 'Hey, Harry, where do I find the stuff on Mrs. Geeson?'

'Be with you in a minute.' He prowled among his files and I sat down at a small desk. Constance sat on the edge and swung a nyloned leg.

'Need any help?'

'Maybe.' I unfolded the paper with the item. 'This squib here, where's this chick been playing?'

'Susan?' She knew who was meant as well as I did. 'The Purple Orchid, mostly. You know the place, classy joint down on the Island. Good food, good wines, excellent entertainment, and a nice, private layout in the back.' She sounded as cynical as a newspaper reporter could be. I nodded.

'That's what I thought. Thornedyke runs it, doesn't he?'

'That's right. Pays plenty of protection too from what I can make out.' She seemed about to say something else, but Harry came over then with a couple of big folders and I set to work.

Constance hovered over me for a while then, knowing I wouldn't spill anything until I was ready, took off on her own private business. I sat and smoked and read the clippings, making notes now and again, and slowly building up a picture of the missing woman.

It didn't help.

Either the papers didn't know or, more likely, she hadn't been in print before her marriage. There was plenty of coverage for the wedding, some background for the Colonel, and a sickly write-up about the new bride. There were pictures of the children too, Stephan looking more human than when I had last met him. I turned back and read about the accident. The Colonel's first wife had died instantly when her car had smashed against a pylon at sixty miles an hour. Cause of death was, as Marvin had told me, a burst front tyre. Even to me there was no suspicion of foul play. The insurance people would have covered that possibility.

I stayed in the morgue for over an hour, and when I left I was little the wiser. The thing I had hoped to find just wasn't in the files, but I hadn't given up trying.

At a bar I changed a dollar into nickels and shut myself in a phone booth. Half an hour later I contacted the party I wanted.

A smooth voice asked me to wait, and I could hear the low mutter of conversation as an order was relayed to someone else. I waited, lighting a cigarette and trying not to feel the cold, which had turned my feet into a couple of cakes of river ice. A voice echoed in my ear.

'Yes?'

'Colonel Geeson?'

'Yes, yes, what is it?' He was impatient—I had called him away from a bridge session at his club.

'Lantry here, Colonel.'

'Lantry?' His hesitation was as phony as a three-dollar bill. 'Ah, yes I recall the name now. Well, have you found her yet?'

I smiled at his innocence.

'Not yet, Colonel. This case isn't as simple as I thought. I need some more help. Would you instruct your lawyers to give it to me?'

'What!' For a moment I thought that he was going to choke. 'My lawyers! Really Lantry, is this necessary?'

'No,' I snapped. My feet were getting even colder and my temper was running out. 'I can do it the hard way. I can ask around and leave a trail of speculation, or I can grease a few palms and get unreliable information. I can act like an undercover man, or I can be open about it. What reason have you for refusing to assist me?'

'I came to you, Lantry,' he said, and I could imagine how he looked, 'because I didn't want to be bothered with trivial details. As yet, you've done nothing but make a nuisance of yourself. I—'

'Hold it, Colonel.' I dragged at my cigarette and forced myself to remember that I needed his money. 'I'm not bothering you. All I want you to do is to phone your lawyers and tell them to assist me. Unless they hear from you they'll throw me out, and rightly so. I can get the information I want from the police if I have to, but—'

This time it was my turn to be interrupted. 'Not the police, Lantry.' He seemed almost to be scared of the word. 'I want no publicity, understand? Just find my wife, that's all I ask you to do.'

'That's what I intend doing,' I said. 'And I want to do it fast. Well?'

'I'll phone them. You know who they are?'

'You tell me.'

'Wendle, Wendle, and Wayne. They have offices on—'

'I'll find them. Incidentally, Colonel, just for the record, were you at home when your wife left?'

'No.'

'No?' I didn't have to ask the question in my voice.

'No, Lantry, I wasn't. I'd been at my club playing poker with a few old friends, and when I returned she had gone.' He hesitated. 'At least I assume that she had gone.'

'Don't you know?'

'We had separate rooms,' he explained. 'It was late and I didn't look in at her. She could have gone any time during the night.'

I nodded. It made sense.

'One other point, Colonel,' I said gently. 'That ten thousand dollars you offered for finding your wife. Does it matter if she's dead or alive?'

For a long moment he didn't answer. The wires hummed and outside the booth a waiting client stamped his feet with impatience and cold.

'Dead or alive?' He didn't seem to know how to put it. 'What makes you think that she is dead?'

'I don't. I'm only covering myself.'

'I see.' Relief? I didn't know, but I'd have taken a bet that he was sweating. 'Find her, Lantry.' Now he had lost his casualness and made no attempt to hide his desperation. 'Find her and I'll pay you the ten thousand.'

It was the only answer I could expect.

I hung up and thumbed through the phone book for the address of the lawyers. I found it, a swanky office off Fifth Avenue, and memorised it. I nodded to the half-frozen character waiting outside and, because the

Colonel was paying expenses, I took a cab.

The firm of Wendle. Wendle, and Wayne occupied a full floor of a big new office block where money had been spent to the best advantage. I rode up in a plush, lined elevator, walked across an acre of carpet, and let the thick pile slow me to a halt before a receptionist who was just a little too perfect to be true. She glanced at me, a quick, professional glance which checked every item of clothing I wore, X-rayed my wallet, and took a shrewd guess at the size of my bank account.

She wasn't impressed.

'Yes?'

'My name is Lantry, Mike Lantry.' I gave her one of my personal cards. 'Mr. Wendle, or someone, is expecting me.'

'Indeed?' She didn't call me a liar, but her eyes did it for her. She flipped the switch of an intercom.

'Mr. Wendle. There is a person, a Mr. Lantry, outside to see you. He says that you are expecting him.'

The machine crackled in a language all of its own, and she lost her supercilious expression.

'Yes, sir.' She looked at me. 'Mr. Wendle will see you now.' She pointed towards a door to one side of the desk. 'If you will enter his private office, he will join you in a moment.'

I nodded, flicked ash over the carpet, and walked towards the indicated door.

Wendle—I never did find out just how he stood in relation to the others in the firm—was a surprisingly young man for a lawyer. That put him around fifty, with the regular touch of grey at his temples, the pink, well-massaged jowls, the controlled paunch, and the too-bright teeth. He shook my hand, neither trying to impress me with his strength nor disgust me with his weakness, and waved me to a chair.

'Did the Colonel phone you?' I looked around for an ash tray, and he pushed one towards me. I parked my butt and was ready for business.

'He did.' Wendle coughed with a lawyer's innate caution and sat down behind his desk. He rested his elbows on the polished wood, his fingers held steeple-wise, and his eyes staring at me from either side as though he were a bird looking at a worm.

'So you know who I am and why I am here. Suppose you tell me what you've discovered so far?'

'That can be told in one word—nothing.'

'Nothing at all?' I frowned. 'Look, I don't want to tell you your business, but I assume that the Colonel has been through the usual routine. Or you did it for him. Yes?'

'Yes,' he admitted. 'The Colonel contacted us the morning after she disappeared. We've covered the ground pretty well, Mr. Lantry. The hospitals, the morgue, the usual thing. No sign of her.'

'How about the stores where she had a charge account? The bank? Places like that?'

'We know our job,' he said dryly. 'When I say that we have found no trace of her, I mean that literally.'

I nodded and lit a fresh cigarette. Wendle obviously knew what he was talking about, and if the missing woman had stopped off for clothes or money, he would know about it. It would be wasting time for me to cover the same ground. I blew a thin streamer of smoke towards the ceiling.

'A question, Mr. Wendle. Why hasn't the Colonel informed the police of his wife's absence?'

Wendle shrugged, saying nothing, and silence began to close in around us. I tried again.

'Tell me, do you approve of the Colonel employing me to find the missing woman?'

'The firm recommended you,' he said quietly.

'The firm? Not you, personally? Why?'

'I think that all this is wholly unnecessary, Mr. Lantry. It wouldn't be the first time that a young and beautiful woman has run away from a, shall we say, old husband? My belief is that she will contact him as soon as she needs money. To employ you, or to inform the police, is merely to arouse a lot of undesirable publicity which the Colonel will be the first to regret.'

'Perhaps. But if the firm recommended me, it must be confident of my discretion.' I leaned forward. 'Now, Mr. Wendle, just how badly does the Colonel want to find his wife?'

He took his time over that one, studying the tips of his fingers as though he had never seen them before.

'Mrs. Geeson is a young and beautiful woman,' he said slowly, as if that explained everything, which maybe it did. 'Naturally, he wants to find her.'

'Let me put it a different way,' I said. 'The Colonel married her, sure, but his son Stephan is carrying a torch for her. He says that he knew her first. What made her marry the old man instead of his son?'

'Stephan has no money of his own,' explained Wendle. 'His mother left certain sums in trust, but they are controlled during the lifetime of his father at the Colonel's discretion. I assume, if you must have an answer, that Mrs. Geeson saw on which side her bread was buttered.'

'Which means that you don't think much of the Colonel's lady.' I gave him a man to man look and he thawed a little.

'We made investigations, of course. I made them myself, checking her background and things like that. Unfortunately, Mrs. Geeson did not have too good a reputation.'

'Did not?' That past tense again. I wondered if people always spoke of absent people as though they were dead. He didn't let it throw him.

'Did not,' he repeated firmly. 'Since her marriage she has been most circumspect.'

'The Colonel knew about her? About her reputation?'

'Naturally.'

'And still he married her?'

'Unfortunately, yes.' Wendle coughed again. 'There's an old saying, you know.'

'No fool like an old fool.' I nodded, this wasn't getting me anywhere. 'All this is very interesting, but it isn't of much help.' I paused, then sprang the sixty-four-dollar question. 'Who gets the money if the Colonel should die?'

I didn't get an answer and I wasn't surprised. Lawyers are closer than oysters when it comes to keeping secrets, and the disposal of the Geeson fortune would be the secret of the year. I rephrased the question.

'Let me put it this way. If Mrs. Geeson were to be found dead, who would benefit?'

'No one. There is a little insurance, of course, but the Colonel is hardly in need of that.'

'A little? How much?'

'A hundred thousand dollars.' He dismissed it as though it were a couple of cents. 'I handled the policy, the normal thing: she named her husband as benificiary.'

'And the Colonel, what if he should die?'

'I beg your pardon?'

'Look,' I said patiently. 'Let's play a game called suppositions. I do the supposing and nothing we say will be repeated outside of this room. Supposing the Colonel should die before his wife? Well?'

'Then the fortune, aside from certain trust funds, would go to her.'

'And if he should die after her?'

'Stephan, as the eldest child, would inherit.'

'I see.' I frowned down at the polished surface of the desk. 'So, if the old man should die, his wife would collect—but good.' I looked at him. 'I know that a marriage invalidates any will made prior to the marriage. But is there any way in which a man could cut his wife out of his estate?'

'If good cause were to be found,' admitted Wendle reluctantly. 'It could be done, in this state at least, but only on good grounds.'

'Such as?'

'Desertion. Adultery. Wilful neglect of wifely duties.' He shrugged. 'On this matter as on any other the law is vague. Much would depend on prior circumstances, witnesses, and actual proof. Such a will would be certain to be contested.' He stared at me. 'What are you getting at, Lantry?'

'Nothing, just collecting answers.' I smiled at him and he seemed to relax. 'You said that you had the job of checking her background. Did you find anything?'

'Such as what?'

'Such as previous husband, children, divorce, police record, the usual thing. Well, did you?'

'No. She had lived on the fringe of the law and worked in a night club, but that was really nothing against her. There was one spot of bother down in Florida when a club was raided and she was fined, but she was only sixteen at the time and it wasn't important.'

'I see.' I looked at him. 'What was her name before she married?'

'Hartridge. Mona Hartridge.'

'Born?'

'New Jersey.' He rose from behind his desk. 'I'm afraid that's all I can tell you, Mr. Lantry. Please let me know of any future developments, and if there is any way in which I can help you don't fail to ask.' He smiled at me, waiting for me to get to my feet. I had one more question.

'Her bank statements. Can I see them?'

'No.'

No politeness now, no desire to help, no nothing but a flat refusal. He held out his hand.

'What do you intend doing next, Mr. Lantry?'

'The usual thing. Why?'

'No reason, just curiosity.' He held out his hand. 'Good afternoon, Mr. Lantry.'

I took the hint and shook his hand.

We left it at that.

Outside it was snowing, a thin drift of white powder which turned to slush as it hit the pavements and sidewalks. I glanced at my wristwatch and then up at the darkening sky. A blind match-pedlar drifted past, his stick rapping on the sidewalk, and I dropped two bits into his tray, remembering the time when I had lain for six weeks in a darkened ward, not knowing whether I should ever be able to see again. Memory of that time always gives me the cold shivers, so I stepped into a bar to warm myself.

While there I did some more phoning. First to the Blue Star Company to check on Marvin's tale. He had told me the truth, no car and driver had been sent to the Colonel's house during the time in question. I dropped more nickels into the slot and rang my stooge at City Hall. I call him my stooge because he's always ready to earn a fast buck, and it saves me lots of time whenever I want to check the records. I gave it to him straight.

'Fred? Mike here. Check back on a Mona Hartridge,

born anywhere up to thirty years ago somewhere in New Jersey. If it will help you any, she's now known as Mrs. Geeson. Got that?'

'Yeah,' his voice sounded eager. 'Something cooking?'

'I wouldn't know.' Fred was sixty years old, lived on a diet of pulp magazines, and only liked his job as night-watchman because it enabled him to carry a gun. He thought that I lived on the thin edge of the law and wanted the information for purposes of blackmail. I didn't discourage him, because it stopped him talking and made him eager to dig up dirt.

'New Jersey.' Fred sounded disappointed. 'It'll take time, chief. You want it fast?'

'Not so fast that you muff the job. Cover her both ways from the middle. Got it?'

'Sure. Worth a fin?'

'Do it good and there's a sawbuck in it for you.' I gave him a knowing chuckle. 'Ten dollars. Fred, think of the magazines you can buy with that.'

'Gee, double rates.' He sniffed and I knew that he would work at it all night. 'Phone in as usual?'

'Yeah.'

I hung up and returned to the bar. I was still cold, and a couple of whiskies didn't do much to warm me.

So I had some more.

After a while I remembered Pug, so phoned the Around the Clock Agency, a place which took and kept messages for their subscribers. I gave them my code number and the girl checked back for me.

'Two messages,' she said. 'One at eleven forty-five from a Mr. Smith, who wants you to call him back. The other at four-fifteen from a Pug Berson.'

'Pug?' Smith I discounted. I knew him as a fellow who hoped to collect a little money from me, and I'd pay him as soon as I got time to post him a cheque. Pug was different. 'Read it,' I said.

'Message begins,' said the voice. 'I've found her. Come to Grimson's place down on East Side. 1147 East Thirty-Second Street.' Message ends.

Pug had hit the jackpot.

CHAPTER SIX

Grimson's place was a run-down tavern down in the poorer quarter of town. I pushed through the doors and into an atmosphere composed of equal parts of cigarette smoke and stale breath, and after the cold cleanness of the evening it almost made me gag. I stepped to the bar, ordered a drink for the benefit of the house, then looked for Pug.

I found him with a blonde occupying a secluded booth and having himself one hell of a time.

'Here he is.' He pushed the blonde from around his neck and grinned at me. 'Mike, meet Francy. Francy, this is Mike Lantry.'

'Please to meet you,' she simpered and looked hopeful. I waved to the self-styled waiter and had him bring some drinks and, while he was getting them, waited for Pug to break the news.

He took his time about it and I lost patience.

'You phoned me,' I reminded. 'Well?'

'Yeah.' He blinked as if I'd startled him. 'That's right, Mike, I did, didn't I?'

'You did.' I didn't want to talk business in front of Francy and Pug didn't seem to want to send her away.

So I did it for him.

'Beat it, sister.'

'What!' She looked annoyed. 'Say—'

'Take a powder.'

'Wait a minute, Mike.' Pug shook his head. 'This is her.'

'Who?'

'The dame you sent me after.'

Maybe I was the one who was crazy. I took a second look at her, paying attention to the bone structure of her face and the slant of her eyes. It didn't add up.

'Not her,' said Pug. 'I mean she isn't the one, but she knows her.'

It was getting confused and I took a drink to straighten things out. While I was doing it, Pug explained.

'Francy knew her,' he said. 'Way back when they worked together at the same club. That right, Fran?'

'Maybe,' she said primly.' 'That depends.'

'Depends on what?' I knew but I asked just the same. She made a gesture with thumb and forefinger. I shrugged.

'Look,' she said, and now she was all business. 'When Pug showed me the photograph, I recognised her as someone I used to work with. That good enough?'

'Maybe. Where? When?'

'Three, four years ago. She was a singer then working the smokers and concerts.' Francy looked as if she had a bad taste in her mouth. 'You know the sort of thing. Well, Rhoda, that's what she called herself then, was always on about breaking out and getting herself on top.' She smiled without humour. 'We all talked like that; some of us made it, others—'

I didn't need her to go into details.

'Do you know where she is now?'

'No.'

'Do you know her friends? What happened to her?'

'No.'

'That's a great help.' I looked at Pug and he lost his self-satisfied grin.

'What's the matter, Mike? It's a lead, can't you take it from there?'

'Sure.' I said tiredly. 'So you meet someone who used to know someone four years ago. Hell. Pug, I know where she was three days ago.'

'So it's no dice?' Fran looked disappointed. I shook my head.

'No dice, but have a drink all the same.'

I held out my hand while she was having it, and Pug gave me the photograph. I stared at it, trying to imagine the woman she appeared to be four years ago when she was riding the cheap circuits. She must have had a tough time.

'Tell me about her,' I said suddenly. 'You called her Rhoda. Was that her real name?'

'Stage name. She was born in some hick town way out West, Texas, I think.'

'Texas?' I frowned at her. 'Sure it wasn't New Jersey?'

'Texas. I remember because her folks died while she was working with me, and she couldn't raise the fare to go and see them buried.'

'I see. You never did know her real name?'

'No.' Fran shrugged. 'You know how it is. A dame runs into a little trouble and changes her name. Or she's a flop and changes it for luck. Or maybe she was wanted, or something like that. Hell, what's in a name, anyway?'

'Nothing. What was the last you heard of her?'

'She got a spot in the Purple Orchid. I never saw her after that.'

'See!' Pug was triumphant. 'I told you that I'd seen her running around with Thornedyke's crowd. All we've got to do now is to go to the Purple Orchid and find her.'

'Just like that?' I shrugged. 'Thanks, Fran, you've been a help. Here.' I slipped her twenty dollars, not for what she had said, but because she obviously needed it. She didn't bother to argue, but her eyes did her thanking for her.

I got up from the table and Pug looked at me.

'We going somewhere?'

'We aren't. I am. Look, be at my office at ten tonight. I'm expecting a visitor. I may be a little late; if I am hold him until I get there.' I looked at Pug. 'By hold him I don't mean knock him out. Be gentle, understand?'

'Sure, Mike.' He grinned at me. 'I'll be as gentle as a baby.'

'See that you are.' I looked at Fran. 'Do me a favour, pal. See that he gets there. Right?'

She nodded and I left, pushing my way through the

smoke and out into the cold evening air.

It was getting dark.

At seven o'clock I arrived at the Purple Orchid. It was a big, sprawling place outside the city limits, but within its jurisdiction. Once it had been a respectable, colonial-type mansion, but now, while still outwardly respectable, it had been dolled up with coloured lights, a superb dance floor, a good floor show, and a complete gambling layout in the upstairs rooms. No one was supposed to know about the gambling, but it was the kind of secret which everyone but the police knew about. They either didn't know or didn't want to know, and the betting was that they didn't want to know.

A set-up like that must have paid off in plenty of heavy money for protection, and rumour had it the Chief of Police was busy building himself a house which normally he could never have paid for in a hundred years.

I didn't worry about that.

I stood looking at the big centre sign of the flower which gave the place its name. It threw a brilliant purple light over the snow-covered drive, turning the evergreens into sickly relief and making the coldness of the night seem even colder.

A uniformed negro touched his cap as I approached the doors, his teeth flashing in a mechanical smile of welcome.

'Evening, suh. Cold night.'

'It is.' I nodded towards the almost empty car park. 'Many here yet?'

'Not yet, suh. Too early.'

I grunted something and passed into the warm, scented air of the interior. A hat-check girl smiled at me with professional charm as I gave her my fedora and gabardine. A tuxedoed bouncer who looked like a college graduate valued my suit and then nodded at me as I passed. A second smiled at me, searched my face in case I was a Fed, then stepped aside. I went in search of the bar.

As the doorman had said, it was early yet. A few couples swayed on the floor, keeping indifferent time to the band, and a few early starters leaned on the polished counter of the bar, their drinks in their hands, staring at their reflections in the bar mirror. I slipped on to a stool and ordered Scotch.

I nursed the drink while he fetched my change, then jerked my head towards the ceiling.

'Thornedyke around yet?'

He shrugged, not answering.

'I asked you a question,' I said loudly. 'Do I get an answer?'

'You want him?'

'That's the general idea.' I sipped at the drink. 'Send word, will you.'

'Name?'

'Lantry. Mike Lantry.' I didn't smile. 'He may know me.'

He shrugged again and moved down towards the end of the bar. A man stood there, not a customer, and after a while he came towards me.

'Trouble, Lantry?' He was well-spoken, he kept his voice low and, to all outward appearances, he was a gentleman. I knew better.

'No.' This time I did smile. 'I'm in a little difficulty and I thought that Thornedyke might be able to help me out. Just as a favour, you understand.'

'I see.' He looked thoughtful. 'Just like that, eh?'

'Just like that.'

'I'll go see if he can spare you some time,' he decided. 'Unless I can help you?'

'Thanks, but no.' I looked at my wristwatch. 'Sorry to rush you, but I'm pressed for time.'

He nodded and left, walking smoothly towards the rear of the building. I stared after him, wondering how any heel could manage to look so much like a decent citizen. I sighed and ordered another drink.

A woman, dressed in a low-cut gown and with a professional smile of welcome, slipped on to the seat next to mine and stared at me. A hostess, probably working on a percentage basis. I smiled back at her.

'Drink?'

'Please.' She made signs to the bartender and he set something before her. It cost enough to have been refined gold, but it was probably cold tea. She drank it and looked at me.

'Look,' I said, 'do you have to earn money the hard way? Just tell me what you reckon on earning by the way of drinks from me and I'll just pay you. That way we'll both get the benefit.'

'Smart guy,' she said without expression.

'I've worked behind a bar,' I explained. 'Don't get me wrong, sister. I'm working.'

'So am I, and if you want to talk to me you'll have to pay for the privilege—my way.'

I grinned and waved towards the bartender and bought some more cold tea. It made me shudder to see her drink it, but what the hell? How else could she be expected to sit and drink all night every night?

'What's your name, honey?'

'Georgette, and yours?'

'Lantry. Mike Lantry. If you're ever in trouble let me know.' I gave her one of my business cards. She took it and frowned.

'Might come in handy at that. You said you were working?'

'That's right.' I took out the photograph. 'Ever see her before?'

'Sure,' she said, then hesitated. 'That is—'

'Mrs. Geeson, and you knew her before she was married.' She hadn't told me, but I was telling her. 'Don't try to kid me you've never seen her, Georgette, it's written all over your face. Well?'

'So I knew her, so what?'

'So she's missing and I want to find her.' I put away the print. 'That is, her husband wants to find her. Nothing wrong, you understand, but if she's sick or needs money or anything like that, he'd like to know.' I sipped at my drink. 'Know where she is?'

'No.'

'A pity.' I took out a packet of cigarettes, gave her

one, then lit them both with my lighter. 'How well did you know her?'

'I've seen her around.' She was lying and I knew it, but there was nothing I could do about it. Either she wanted to talk or she didn't. It was as simple as that.

'Look,' I said confidentially. 'You know how it is. I'm on expenses and can afford to spread a little. Now if you should suddenly remember where she might be, you could phone me and receive a birthday package in return.'

'How big a package?'

'Five hundred dollars.' I blew a smoke ring. 'Think it over, Georgette. You have my card.' I smiled at her then turned as the well-dressed heel came towards me.

She nodded, slipping quickly from the stool, and I stared into the enigmatic eyes of the messenger.

'Mr. Thornedyke can spare you a few minutes, Lantry,' he said evenly. 'Follow me, please.'

I nodded and followed him towards the back rooms.

Thornedyke was a businessman. He had assessed crime, found that it paid, and then gone in for it in a big way. He wore expensive suits, took care of his account, and made sure that he couldn't be hurt. He stared at me as I entered his office.

'Lantry. What can I do for you?'

'Answer a few questions.' I sat down opposite him and looked at him across his wide desk. 'Nothing personal in this, Thornedyke, but I'm in a spot and maybe you could help me out.' I paused, he didn't say anything, so I continued.

'I'm looking for Mrs. Geeson. She used to work here and I wondered if you'd heard from her.'

'Mrs. Geeson?'

'Norma. You know the dame I mean.'

'I know,' he admitted. 'What about her?'

'When she worked here, did she run around with many boyfriends?'

'I wouldn't know,' he said coldly. I tried again.

'Susan drops a little money from time to time upstairs, doesn't she? Does the boy come here too?'

'Talking out of turn, aren't you, Lantry?'

'Quit acting the gentleman,' I snapped. 'I know you, Thornedyke, and you know me. All I'm interested in is finding Mrs. Geeson. What you do upstairs doesn't worry me. Now, can you help me or can't you?'

'I can give you some advice,' he said evenly. 'Take your nose out of Norma's business and keep it out. If you don't, there's liable to be one less shamus dirtying up the city.'

'Thanks for nothing.' I stared at him and he lowered his eyes. 'What's Norma to you, Thornedyke?'

'Nothing.'

'What *was* she to you, then?'

'Nothing.' He spread his hands a little. 'She worked here, but a lot of girls do that. She left here to get married, so do most of the others, I run a clean place, Lantry, and don't you forget it.'

'So you run a clean place,' I said. 'The police seem to think so, anyway. But never mind that. Have you seen her since she left?'

'No.'

'Know where she might be?'

'No.'

'Any idea of a secret boyfriend? Someone she might have run off with?'

It was getting monotonous and I was getting tired. I rose to my feet and dropped one of my cards on the desk. 'Thanks for seeing me. If you should see her or learn anything, let me know. Right?'

'I'll think about it,' he said. He reached for the card then paused as the telephone rang. He picked up the receiver.

'Yes? That's right. Yes.' His eyes sharpened as he looked at me. 'Keep talking.'

I moved towards the door and he gestured to me.

'Hold it, Lantry. I might have something for you.'

He clamped the receiver to his ear again, and listened some more. When he put down the instrument, he looked thoughtful.

'Well?' I stared at him. 'What have you got for me?'

'She had a friend who might know something.' He frowned. 'I can't remember her name, but it'll come to me. Look, leave it with me for now. I'll do what I can and phone you later. Okay?'

I nodded.

CHAPTER SEVEN

Downstairs the place was beginning to fill up with pleasure-hungry customers. I looked for Georgette but couldn't find her, and stood for a moment figuring on what to do next. I still had some spare time, so I decided to hang around for an hour and see what cropped up.

Susan cropped up.

I spotted her as she came through the inner doors. She was dressed in a silver thing which hugged her like a second skin and, against all the time-worn beauties, she looked as fresh and as radiant as a breath of spring. A man was with her, some uptown playboy, and I watched them as he steered her towards a table.

He didn't like my joining them.

'Miss Geeson?' I sat down as she turned towards me. 'Remember me?'

'Mr. Lantry.' She wasn't pleased or annoyed or anything. She looked even more tired than when I had seen her last, and I wondered what it was about money that seemed to spoil everyone who touched it. Her escort, a smooth, well-dressed man fresh from Harvard, looked towards me.

'Is this man bothering you, Susan?'

'No,' she said. 'Forget it.'

'If he's worrying you—' He let his voice fade into silence as he gave me the eye. I didn't let it bother me.

'He's not offending me, John.' She sounded as if she was too tired to care.

'May I have a word with you, Miss Geeson?' I looked at her escort. 'Privately?'

'If you wish.' She looked at John and he took the hint. I watched him go over to the bar.

'Fiancé?'

'No.'

'Playing tonight?'

'That's my business.' She fumbled for a cigarette and I passed her one of my own. She hesitated before taking it, then shrugged and allowed me to give her a light. I snapped shut the lighter and became serious.

'I'm not just making noises, Miss Geeson, or should it be Susan?'

'Why not?'

'I hate being formal. Well, Susan, you know that Norma used to work here, don't you?'

'Did she?'

'You know she did.' I dragged at my cigarette. 'The point I'm making is this: do you come here to lose money because of that?'

I'd startled her. I could tell it from the way she sucked in her breath and the fingers of the hand holding the cigarette tightened so that she crushed the paper. I waited for her to recover her calm.

'I think that you're a fool,' she said deliberately. 'An ill-mannered fool at that.' The contempt in her voice could have been cut with a knife.

'Thinking is your privilege,' I said lightly. 'But remember this, Susan. I'm employed to find your step-mother. I'm going to do that. If I can help you on the side, I'll do it, but I'm not going to cover up for you unless you come clean.'

'I don't know what you're talking about.'

'I think that you do,' I said. 'I think that you've a pretty shrewd idea where your step-mother might be. Think me a fool if you like, but don't make the mistake of thinking that Thornedyke's a fool too. He isn't, believe me he isn't, and that boy plays for keeps.'

'Do you have any idea of what you are saying?' She crushed out the cigarette and rose to her feet. 'Really, Mr. Lantry, I have a very poor opinion of your intelligence after what you have said. May I ask you to stop from bothering me?'

'You may.' I stood up and watched her rejoin her escort. He glared at me and I smiled back. I wasn't worried; the more people who thought that I was a fool, the better I like it. People get careless when they think they are the only clever ones.

But I didn't like to think of Susan getting mixed up with a rat like Thornedyke.

A glance at my watch told me that it was time to get moving, so I went to the hat-check girl to collect my hat and coat. She took her time finding them, so much time that I began to wonder whether or not she'd sold them or given them away to the deserving poor.

Finally I collected my belongings and stepped out of the club into a swirling mass of snow.

It was quite dark now and the glare of the neons made the falling flakes seem like something out of this world. I stamped my feet to keep them warm while the doorkeeper whistled for a cab.

It slid to a halt before the doors, the doorkeeper opened the back door, and I ducked inside out of the storm. The door slammed shut behind me and the cab started with a jerk which threw me against something soft and yielding. Startled, I reached for the light switch.

'Hold it!' Something hard jabbed into my stomach. 'We don't need no lights.'

I didn't answer. Even before he spoke I'd started for my gun, realised that I couldn't get it out in time, and dropped my hand. My companion chuckled.

'Now you're getting smart. Just sit down and take it nice and easy.' His voice had a peculiar purring sound, as though he were a cat licking his chops over a bowl of cream. I tried to place it, but it was one I hadn't heard before. I sat very still as he patted my clothing and lifted the Browning from the underarm holster.

'Got it, Lefty?' The driver, a dim shadow against the snow-covered windscreen, half-twisted his head as he tried to do two things at once. The man called Lefty snarled as the cab skidded.

'Watch your driving. I've got his gat. Here.' He dropped it over the front seat while I cursed myself for all sorts of a fool.

It was so obvious that I could have kicked myself. The delay in getting my hat and coat, plenty of time for the hat-check girl to pass the word that I was on the way out. The whistled signal from the doorkeeper and the car, which in the snow I had mistaken for a cab.

'Thornedyke put you boys up to this?' I kept my voice as casual as though I was asking for a match.

'Maybe.' Lefty gave his purring chuckle and his eyes gleamed in the darkness with an unusual glitter.

'Was it?'

'Don't get lippy, pal. It ain't healthy.'

'So it was Thornedyke. What gives?'

'Just a little ride, pal. We like your company so much that we want more.' The purr whispered in the confines of the car like an animal noise of anticipation. 'Nothing serious, so don't get all upset and do anything to make me shoot you. I'd hate to do that. It would mess up the cushions something terrible.' He chuckled again and I recognised his type.

A goon. A trigger-happy gunsel out on a job and enjoying himself. A man as liable to pull the trigger of the gun pointed at my stomach as to blow his nose. I relaxed and grinned into the darkness.

'That's good news. Thornedyke must think more of me than I guessed.'

A hand swept from out of the darkness. A big hand wearing a heavy ring. It dashed across my mouth and I tasted blood from my split lips. Instinctively I lunged at the dim shape, knotting my fist and slamming it towards where I thought his throat would be. I missed, bruising my knuckles against the side of the car, and the gun barrel jabbed into my stomach with enough force to make me gag.

'Try that again, pal, and I'll blow you wide open. This ain't no stick of rock I'm holding.'

'Cut the jabber, Lefty,' snapped the driver. 'Give it to him.'

'And spoil the car covers?'

'To hell with that. Get it over with.'

'Pipe down, Spike,' purred Lefty. 'I'm enjoying this.'

I wasn't. I'd been held up before, slugged before, and even taken for a ride a couple of times, but I still hadn't learned to like it. I never would learn to like it, not while my life hung on an idiot's whim. And Lefty was an idiot, a gun-crazy moron. I'd met his type before.

'How much are you boys getting for this?' I kept my voice casual. Lefty sniggered.

'Hear that, pike? The man wants to know how much we're getting for this.'

'I heard him,' growled Spike. 'Get on with it and cut the jabber.'

'You cut your jabber,' snarled Lefty with a sudden change of temper. 'Your job is to drive this crate, not give me lip.'

'Yes, Lefty,' said the driver humbly, and I guessed that he was as scared of the moron as I was.

That's right. Scared.

An idiot with a gun is the same as a hophead or a drunk—unpredictable. They'll kill a man for the laughs or for a lift of an eyebrow, or just for the fun of hearing the gun go 'bang'. My life was hanging by a thread and I knew it.

'Listen,' I said. 'I don't know what you've been offered, but I'll double it. Is it a deal?'

'Did you hear that, Spike?' Lefty had recovered his good humour and his purr. 'The man's offering us money. He's scared.' The gun jabbed at me. 'Are you scared?'

'Sure he's scared,' said Spike hastily. 'How much money have you got, pal?'

'A hundred and fifty dollars. Will you take it and let me go?'

'Sure,' said Lefty quickly.' He lied and I knew it. 'Pass the coin and we'll forget all about it. Right?'

'Right.'

I twisted, wriggling on the seat as if I were trying to get out my wallet. While I wriggled I stared at Spike. As I'd hoped, he was more interested in what was going on behind him than on his job. Normally that wouldn't have mattered, but things weren't normal. The roads were a sheet of freezing snow, the windscreen was clogged with it, and vision was down to a few feet.

I grunted, swept down my hand and felt the cold metal of the gun barrel smack against my palm. With my shoulder I hit the light switch and while the light blazed on, I wrenched at the automatic. Lefty squealed as the trigger guard scraped his fingers, and then the weapon came free. I swung at him just as the car skidded and left the road.

The motion ruined my aim so that I dug a hole in the cushion, the impact jarring the gun from my hand. Lefty yelled as I struck at him, kicking and chopping for his throat, then the car jolted to a halt and Spike joined in the fight.

He grabbed up the Browning and swung at me, leaning over the back seat. I saw his eyes, wild with fear and terror, and I saw the little round hole which would soon be spitting lead and flame. With fifteen shots in the magazine, with me tangled in the back of the car and with only two feet between us, he couldn't miss.

I jerked at the door handle and fell out into the snow as lead whined through the space where my head had been.

Almost I made it. Almost I got free into the snow and darkness. Then I tripped over something, fell head-first against a tree, and by the time I had shaken the stars out of my eyes they were all over me.

Through a red haze of pain I felt the impact of blows on my head and shoulders and, coupled with the soggy impact, the sound of a snarling purr, which was Lefty getting his own back. I doubled, shoved my head into my lap, locked the fingers of both hands over the back of my neck, and brought my heels up behind my buttocks. Like a ball I rolled towards an incline I had noticed when leaving the car. It had stopped on the verge of a slope and I hoped to be able to roll down it before I was beaten to a jelly.

It was a close thing.

They could hurt me, but not too seriously, my arms and legs protected the weaker portions of my body. I felt the slam of blows against my kidneys, the thrust of feet against my sides, and the pounding of something hard against the top of my head. Then, as if they had grown tired and wanted to get it over, I heard the whistle of air as something cut through it towards me. I jerked, felt myself begin to fall, then the top of my head seemed to split wide open into a great, black, star-lined hole.

I fell into it and kept on falling.

I never did reach the bottom.

CHAPTER EIGHT

I was lying on something soft and cold, wet and chilling. I rested there, feeling the cold seep into my bones. It didn't seem so much cold as numbing. I lay there for a long while, just resting, just trying to get the throbbing out of my head and the sickness out of my stomach. Resting didn't help, so I decided to open my eyes.

It took a long time.

Finally I prised them open and stared up at the snow-covered branches of a tree. They hung above me, very beautiful with their covering of fleecy-white snow, then, as I looked, a clot of the white stuff fell towards me and hit me in the face. It was time to move.

The base of my stomach was sore, my legs were sore, my kidneys hurt like hell, and it was painful to move. The backs of my hands were swollen and I had a bruised cheek. The top of my head carried a couple of lumps the size of eggs, and I was so cold that my teeth chattered like the castanets of some Mexican dancing girl.

Other than that I was quite all right.

I looked around me. The goons had probably left

me after I had rolled down the slope. They had gone, and so had their car. Thinking hurt my head and the pain made my thoughts all fuzzy, as though they were wrapped in cotton. I fell flat on my face as I tried to walk up the slope and, before trying again, I grabbed hold of a double handful of the white stuff and rubbed it over my face.

It stung and the cold was something I wanted to get away from, but it helped, and by the time I had crawled to the top my brain was functioning again. I stood on the verge of a road and waited for the traffic which wasn't there. While waiting I walked. I like to think of it as walking, though my trail in the snow was something only a drunk would have emulated. I didn't know where I was or which direction to take, but I knew that if I didn't keep moving I would freeze.

So I kept moving.

I waited for a long time before a car came humming towards me. I waved, even tried to yell, but it did not do any good. The red tail lights seemed to sneer at me as they vanished into the distance. A second car came, then two together, then nothing for a long, long time. I could have wept.

The next pair of headlights to show themselves found me swaying in the middle of the road. The car could stop or not, as the driver chose. If it stopped, I was going to ask for help. If it didn't, I'd be in no condition to do any asking, anyway.

It stopped.

I hobbled towards it and a flashlight beam hit me

straight between the eyes.

'You in trouble, mister?'

'Yeah.' I clung to the edge of the door panel and tried to make my voice sound like a voice. The flash-light beam bothered me, I couldn't see past it, and the driver bothered me too. The voice had been too high-pitched for a man and too resonant for that of a boy. I must have been still pretty fogged from the beating up, because I didn't think of a woman.

She chuckled and lowered the flashlight.

'Why, Mr. Lantry, fancy meeting you!'

'You know me?' I clawed at the door handle.

'Mike!' This time she wasn't trying to be funny. 'Are you hurt?'

'You could say that.' Now I recognised her, Constance Young of the *New York Tribune*. I could have kissed her.

'Get in, Mike, you'll freeze out there.'

'Thanks.' I dragged open the door and almost fell into the vacant seat. I sat, my head between my hands, and the bottle she passed me was what I needed most. It was Scotch, good Scotch at that, and it took me and shook me and warmed me all over. After the third drink, I remembered my manners and passed her a cigarette.

'Trouble, Mike?' She lit the cigarettes with the dash-lighter, and in the glow I could see her eyes, soft and concerned and not a bit afraid. I squinted at myself in the rear-view mirror and was surprised to find that I still looked human.

'Just a little friendly roughhouse.' I felt myself over, not surprised to find that my wallet and gun were among the missing. I took another sip at the bottle.

'Want to tell me about it?'

'No.'

She wasn't annoyed.

'Private business.' I explained. 'I may get around to telling you later.'

'As you wish.' She started the car and drove with easy skill. I stared out of the windows.

'Which way are we going?'

'To town. Why?'

'Nothing.' I'd been walking in the wrong direction. 'What brought you out here?'

'I've been to the Purple Orchid.'

'Alone?'

'No. My escort got drunk, so I ditched him.' She chuckled as she handled the wheel, the tyres humming as they spun through the snow. 'Some men never learn.'

'That's right.' I winced as I touched the bumps on my head. 'You don't look the gambling type to me, Constance. Why the Purple Orchid?'

'No reasons,' she said, and I knew that she was lying. Why I didn't know. I didn't care either.

I finished the cigarette and lit another. In the dim glow of the instrument panel the hand of the speedometer hovered around a nice, safe thirty. I looked at the clock: it had its hands pointing almost to midnight, and sight of it reminded me of the old butler. I shrugged. He would keep.

Half an hour later we swept into town, and Constance looked questioningly at me.

'Where to?'

'Drop me anywhere.'

'Are you crazy? Where shall I take you?'

'Drop me at the office then,' I said. I felt too weak to argue. She shrugged.

'You are crazy. What you need is a hot bath and a good sleep.'

'What I need is a new body and ten million dollars,' I said. 'I'm not going to get either, so I'll have to make do with what I've got. The office.'

'You're a stubborn fool,' she said without emotion. She spun the wheel and headed towards the section of the town where I hang out my shingle. Softly the car pulled up before the tall building in which I hire a single room. She sat, not speaking, her hands resting lightly on the wheel as she waited for me to get out.

'Thanks, Constance,' I said, and I meant it. 'I'll make this up to you some day.'

'Forget it.' She trod on the gas and the engine roared as she slammed the door after me. 'Be seeing you.'

The car droned down the street with a smooth hum of power, and I stood watching it as it swung around a corner. Nice girl, Constance. A very nice girl. She had saved my life.

I turned towards the building and let myself in with my key.

Inside it was dark and I pressed the automatic stair-lights. I couldn't face the long climb up to the tenth floor so I rested my thumb on the elevator call-button and leaned on it. I could hear the bell ringing somewhere down in the basement. It rang for a long, long time and I was almost asleep when I heard the doors clang and the creaking old cage come wheezing up towards me. I took my finger off the button and waited.

The janitor blinked at me. His eyes were red and his clothing rumpled as if he'd just been wakened from sleep.

He glared at me, not liking what he saw, and muttered something as he opened the cage. I stepped inside and jerked my thumb towards the heavens.

'To the tenth, and wait.'

'Wait?'

'That's right. Unless you want to go all the way down again and then up and then down. I shouldn't be long.'

He mumbled something and started the elevator.

It was a long journey. The floors crawled past us as though we were burrowing our way up from the bowels of the earth, empty, devoid of all life and movement. It was cold too, the heaters had been turned off, and I was shivering by the time we reached the tenth floor.

My office was dark and the automatic stair-lights casting a dim glow from the stair well snapped off as I left the cage. I swore and, fumbling in the dark, found the button and switched them on again. As the lights came on, I stepped towards the door of my office, dragging my keys from my pants pocket and running my finger over them to find the right one. I needn't have bothered, the door was unlocked, anyway.

I swung it open and felt for the lights. My fingers hit the switch and I pressed it. For all the good it did I might as well have tried to switch on the Heavenly Choir. No lights. I tried again, clicking the switch. Nothing. I said something and took three long strides towards where I knew the desk to be.

On the second step I tripped over something soft, stumbled and landed heavily on my knees, the top of my head slamming hard against the side of the desk.

For a moment I counted stars. Then I shook my abused skull, made sure that I hadn't bit my tongue in two pieces, then, dragging myself to my feet, I fumbled around until I found the desk-lamp. I switched it on, it lit, and I stared down at what had tripped me.

It was Harmond.

He lay, his sightless eyes staring at the flaked white-wash on the ceiling, one arm doubled beneath him and the other outstretched as though he had tried to grab at something as he fell. A red-rimmed hole stared at me like a third eye, and blood made a soggy mess on the carpet beneath his head.

He was very dead.

I stooped over and touched the skin of his face, then rested my fingers lightly on the great artery in his throat. His skin was cold, clammy, and the artery had long ago lost the pulse of life. I straightened and stared down at the old butler, and his dead eyes stared back at me like the windows of a deserted house.

He had carried a million trays, run a million errands, had served others all his life, and now? Now someone had served him an ounce of lead, had blasted the life from his body, smashed his skull, and left him in red-grey ruin on a dingy carpet in a dingy office in a run-down building.

I felt that I had to have a drink.

The bottle was empty, aside from a few drops clinging to the brown glass, and the few I managed to pry loose didn't do me any good at all. I stared at the bottle, trying to remember when I'd drunk it so low. I hadn't, and with the memory something clicked.

'Pug!'

No answer.

'Pug!' I didn't shout too loud, but loud enough for him to have heard me. Ridiculous really, because if he'd been around I would have seen him. I didn't, but just to make sure I went over the office with a fine-tooth comb. I even looked under the desk. No Pug.

I tossed the bottle back into the drawer, took out my spare gun, checked the loading and slipped it beneath my arm. Outside in the elevator cage I could hear the old janitor sniffle and stamp his feet as he waited for me to finish my business so that he could get back down to the warmth of the boiler room and his inter-rupted sleep.

I left him waiting.

Carefully, so as not to disturb the position of the body, I examined the contents of the dead man's pockets. He had the usual junk, nothing of interest to anyone but himself, and now he wasn't interested in anything anymore.

There was a pawn ticket, a fob watch of gold and with a worn inscription on the back. A wallet with a few bills, some loose change, a dog-eared snapshot of a young woman in a bathing costume, the sort of costume which was all the rage twenty years ago, but now was only worth a laugh. He had some keys, a torn stub from a movie ticket, a roll of peppermints, and a couple of receipts for registered mail. I turned him over, opened the fingers of his hand and pryed loose a scrap of pasteboard. It was one of my own cards, crumpled and dirty, and I stared at it, seeing it as the passport to hell it had become.

I rose and looked down at him, mentally apologising for what had happened and, somewhere, probably in Heaven, perhaps he heard and understood.

I stepped out of the office into the corridor and walked up to the old janitor.

'Did you let anyone in tonight?'

He blinked at me, not fully awake, and I repeated the question. He blinked again and reluctantly tore his thoughts from downstairs and brought them up to the tenth floor.

'Well, now,' he said thoughtfully. 'I did let someone in now that you come to mention it. An old guy.'

'What time?'

'Time?' He had to think that one over. 'Maybe nine or maybe a little later.'

'Did you bring him up here?'

'Yeah.' Life sparkled in his eyes, the animal cunning of a cornered beast who thinks that he sees trouble and wants to avoid it. 'He had one of your cards. He said that you was expecting him and that it would be okay for him to wait. I didn't do nothing wrong, mister. Honest I didn't. I—'

'Yeah, yeah.' I cut short his whining. 'Try and think now. What time did he get here?'

'I told you, about nine, or maybe it was ten, sometime like that.' He was vague. He didn't know. I didn't waste time pressing the point.

'Was he the only one you let in tonight?'

'That's right.'

'You sure?'

'Sure I'm sure!' He licked his bloodless lips. 'I wouldn't let just anyone into the building, mister, you know that. But he had one of your cards, see, and he said that it would be okay for him to wait.'

'I heard you the first time,' I said tiredly. I stood, feeling the cold of the night fight the Scotch, and win. 'Did you shut the door after him?'

'Yeah.'

'Anything else happen? Bell ring or something like that?'

He thought about it, creasing his forehead as he tried to sort dreams from reality, then he nodded.

'That's right. The bell did ring once. I answered it, but there was no one there. I even walked out into the street to make sure.'

I nodded. The old guy was luckier than he knew. The killer had taken a chance, rung the bell, and when the old man had squinted out with his weak eyes had slipped past him into the building without being seen. If the janitor had seen him, or if he had not walked out in the street to see what was doing, the killer would have chalked up a double murder.

That part was simple, but what about Pug?

I knew that big ox and I knew that he wouldn't deliberately let me down. I'd told him to be at the office by ten. He had his own key, so that he needn't have rung the bell to get in. But he was missing, and suddenly I began to get worried about him.

I looked at the old janitor.

'Sure that you've seen no one else tonight?'

'Positive.' He was too. An army could have marched past him, but he found a story and he was sticking to it. I sighed and led him into my office. I pointed to the thing on the floor.

'Recognise him?'

He gulped, his adam's apple bobbing in his scrawny throat, and I had to catch him as his legs buckled beneath him. I sat him in my chair.

'Well?'

'That's him,' he muttered. 'That's the old man I let in tonight.' He stared at me. 'Why did you do it, mister?'

'Are you crazy?' I clamped down on my anger. 'You brought me up here, you've been with me ever since. How could I have killed him?'

He shook his head and I could read the doubt in his eyes.

'He's been shot,' I pointed out. 'Did you hear a shot?'

'No.'

'Did you hear a shot anytime tonight? Anytime at all?'

Again he shook his head, and I knew that he was telling the truth as he knew it. A cannon could have gone off and he wouldn't have known about it, not with him cuddling the boilers down in the basement.

I sighed and reached for the phone.

CHAPTER NINE

Captain Bresholm was one of the few men on the force that I both liked and respected. There were others whom I liked and a few whom I respected, but not the both. Bresholm was different, in that he hadn't let his uniform replace his brains, and he hadn't let a corrupt administration turn him into a crook. He did his job and did it as well as he was allowed, which is different to saying that he did it as well as he could. If sometimes he received a gentle hint from upstairs, he merely shrugged and played the game their way.

He was married with a couple of kids and he liked to eat.

He sat in the customer's chair in my office and stared wooden-faced as the photographers and fingerprint boys did their job. The body had gone, carted away like a hunk of cold meat to the morgue, and I was glad to see it go.

I sat in my own chair and killed cigarettes. My head ached, I couldn't stop shivering, and I felt like death. I wanted a hot bath, hot toddy, and some decent food. I could also do with some sleep.

I hoped that I would be allowed to get them all.

Bresholm snubbed out the butt of a long, thin cigar and snapped his fingers at the police stenographer. The man grunted, closed his book and went outside, where I could hear him stamping his feet.

Bresholm looked at me.

'So, as far as you're concerned, Lantry, this kill is a mystery.'

'Yes.'

'I've heard your story and checked with Constance Young and the janitor, but when you come down to it the story means nothing.'

'I know that,' I said tiredly. 'I could have sprouted wings and flown back from the Purple Orchid. I could have made myself invisible and bumped the old man. Then I could have flown back, beat myself up, and carried on as normal. The reason I killed him, of course, was that I didn't like the way he parted his hair.'

Bresholm wasn't amused.

'You could have returned to the building earlier, let yourself in and bumped the old man,' he pointed out. 'We've only your word for it that you were knocked out and stayed that way for several hours.'

'That's true,' I said. 'Aside from the fact that I was miles away from here, I don't own a car, and I wouldn't have been stupid enough to have killed him in my own office, you've almost got a case.'

'I could hold you on what I've got,' he reminded. 'You knew Harmond would be here tonight, and you're about the only one who did. Your alibi isn't watertight and you know it. He had one of your cards.'

He shrugged. 'Many a man has been burned on less evidence than that.'

'You should know,' I said bitterly. 'Maybe I should have a doctor check my injuries?'

'Wouldn't mean a thing,' he assured cheerfully. He lit a fresh cigar. 'Anyway, it's even simpler than that. You could have set the scene and had an accomplice pull the trigger. See what I mean?'

'Sure. I also had the impression that a man was innocent until he was found guilty.'

He didn't laugh, but then it was nothing to laugh about. Not for a cop who still had some respect for the law. But both he and I knew that assumption was just one of those things. Not that I was worried. Bresholm might take a hint and write off a murder as a suicide, but he wouldn't stand for an innocent man being railroaded to the chair. Not while he knew it, anyway. I leaned towards him.

'Do you think that I killed him?'

'No, Lantry, I don't.' He stared at the tip of his cigar. 'But I've got the impression that you're holding something back. Want to tell me?'

I shrugged. I'm not one of these smart guys who think it clever to run against the cops. I've a living to earn, and I know that I'm allowed to do it on strict sufferance. It would be the easiest thing in the world for Bresholm to have my licence revoked, and without it I'd be hounded by every cop on the beat for every charge in the book. I wouldn't even be allowed to carry a gun.

But against that there was the fact that, to me, a client was protected by professional ethics.

'I'm on a case,' I said briefly. 'Harmond reckoned he knew something and fixed an appointment to see me tonight.' I glanced down at my wristwatch. 'Last night. The rest you know.'

'The Geeson woman?' He smiled at my blank expression. 'Yes, Lantry, I know, not officially, of course, but a thing like that can't be kept secret, not when there's ten million dollars mixed up in it.' He looked at me. 'The information is confidential. Officially I know nothing of the missing woman and I can't do anything about it anyway. It isn't even in my department.'

'So?'

'When people begin asking questions, I can put two and two together. A few hints were dropped in the right places and we did a good job. She hasn't been seen, Lantry.' He puffed at his cigar. 'Why didn't you come to me about it first? I could have saved you a lot of leg work.'

'No thanks. I owe you enough favours as it is.'

'That's what friends are for. Or would there be another reason?'

'Sure. I was hired to do a job not to go around shooting off my big mouth.'

'I see your point.' He nodded and frowned at his cigar. It wasn't drawing well and he had no patience with it. He crushed it out and lit another. 'When are you going to ask me for a job, Lantry? I could use you in Homicide.'

'When I have to.' I grinned at him with the easy familiarity of good friendship. 'You've got too many bosses for my liking, Bresholm. I like to be on my own.'

He shrugged, breathing out clouds of smoke, and stared at me as though he had never seen me before.

'You could be right,' he admitted, and something struggled for expression in his eyes. Struggled and died. A wife and a couple of kids can teach a man to guard his tongue even when he's with friends.

'Am I free to go now?' I rubbed my aching head and glanced at my watch. 'It's past three in the morning and I've had a hard day.'

'You're free.' He rose, brushing a little ash from his suit. 'Drop in at headquarters sometime and sign a statement.' He shrugged. 'Personally, I doubt if we'll find out who did it. No clues, no motive, no nothing. Just one of those things.'

'I'll find him,' I gritted and was surprised at the conviction in my voice. 'I'll find him, and when I do I'll give him to you on a plate—all ready to burn.'

'Maybe.' He looked at me. 'You look all in. How about me dropping you off at home?'

'No thanks.'

'I'll leave a car at the door for a few minutes then. They can drop you off, it's no night for even a dog to be out.'

He was right and I knew it. I smiled.

'Thanks. I'll be right down.'

He nodded and left the room. I could hear his firm,

muscular legs carry him lightly down the stairs. He always walked downstairs, said that it kept him fit, but I didn't feel like following his example.

The elevator took a long time to answer my signal.

The prowl car dropped me off before the apartment house where I live, and the driver waved me goodbye as he slid away from the kerb. The doors were locked, so I had to use my key to get in. The elevator had shut down too, so I had to crawl up to the fifth floor. By the time I arrived my head felt as if it were ready to burst like an overfilled balloon.

I live in one of those small, too-compact apartments where one room doubles up for another. I stripped and filled the bath with water as hot as I could bear. While the tub was filling, I broke open my reserve bottle of Scotch and fed myself a drink. The liquor burned my stomach, but it warmed me and I took another drink before getting into the hot water. I soaked for almost an hour, letting more hot water keep up the temperature, and taking a drink at frequent intervals. When I climbed out of the tub I was as red as a lobster and not quite sober. But the shivering had stopped and I didn't feel as if I was coming down with pneumonia. I got into pyjamas and robe and set some coffee to boil while I fried a couple of eggs.

The food sobered me, the coffee sobered me still more, and for the first time in hours I began to feel really human.

My suit was ready for a trip to the cleaners. Blood, snow, and dirt had made it unfit for wear. I emptied the pockets and tossed it into a corner, then sat down and stared at what I had.

Two receipts for registered mail and one pawn ticket.

Bresholm wouldn't like me having taken them, but what he didn't know wouldn't hurt him. I stared at them for a long time, smoking, drinking, killing time. I was too tired to think straight, and the reaction from what I'd been through was making my thoughts go in circles. I took another drink and tried to concentrate.

The pawn ticket was from a shop down on east side and was for a gold wristwatch. I wondered what Harmond would be doing with a wristwatch when he used a fob timepiece, and then filed it for future reference. The two receipts were both made out to the same address. Harmond, for reasons of his own, had posted a couple of registered envelopes to a Sam Jenkin, who lived at 354 Green Street, down near Greenwich Village. Both had been posted from the same office and they were dated a week apart.

I glanced at my wristwatch and noticed that it was getting near dawn. I pulled the phone towards me and dialed City Hall. I listened as the bell rang and rang and rang at the other end. I was just about to give up when the receiver clicked, and a voice, heavy with sleep and sharp with irritation barked at me.

'Yeah?'

'Fred?'

'Who wants him?'

'Lantry.'

'Mike!' The voice changed, sharpened, became

awake. 'Hell, I didn't recognise your voice. How's it going?'

'Lousy. Did you get it?'

'Sure.' He chuckled as if at a job well done. 'I looked up the records and found what you wanted. Mrs. Geeson was born in New Jersey and had the name of Mona Hartridge. She married the Colonel—'

'Forget it,' I said tiredly. 'Sure there's no mistake?'

'You know me, Mike.' He sounded hurt and I guessed that I'd done him an injustice. 'No soap, huh?'

'You get your money,' I said. 'Thanks, anyway.'

I hung up and stared at the telephone. A hunch? Sure, but this game is full of them. I should have had more sense than not to trust Wendle; a smart lawyer like him would have checked all the angles. So far, my hunch had cost me just ten dollars.

I was still staring at the phone when it rang at me.

'Yes?'

'Mr. Lantry?' It was a man's voice.

'Speaking.'

'Mr. Mike Lantry?' He couldn't seem to get the idea.

'This is him,' I growled. 'What do you want?'

'This is the General Mercy Hospital down near the Bronx. There is a man here, a hit-and-run case, but he had your card in his pocket and we thought that maybe you could identify him.'

He paused, waiting. I didn't say anything.

'Hello?'

'I'm still here,' I said.

'Well, can you?'

'Can I do what?'

'Can you identify him?'

'Look,' I said patiently. 'I have those cards printed by the thousand. I give them to everyone I meet. How the hell can I tell who carries them around with them?' My voice must have echoed my irritation, because he sounded a little hurt.

'I'm sorry, Mr. Lantry, but I thought that maybe this man might be a friend of yours.'

'So he might,' I agreed. 'But it's almost dawn; I haven't slept yet, and the temperature is somewhere around zero. Did you think of that or do you work nights?'

'I work nights,' he admitted, and became a little more human. 'Sorry to bother you, Mr. Lantry, but this is in the nature of an emergency. This man, whoever he is, needs an operation but fast. We'd like to contact his relatives just in case.'

'As bad as that?' Little spiders began running up and down my spine. 'Is he a big man, tough, scarred hands and a boxer's ear?'

'Yes.'

'No wallet, paper, identification?'

'None, that's why I called you.'

'I'm on my way,' I said, and hung up. I hadn't gotten dressed before the phone rang again. This was my busy night.

'Yes?'

'Mike? This is Constance Young. Remember me?'

'Could I ever forget?'

'Thank you. What about that body in your office?'

'Ask the police.'

'I'm asking you, Mike. You know why.'

'You want a story,' I said. 'Don't you reporters ever sleep?'

'I'm on the owl shift,' she sounded amused. 'If I drop over will you talk about it?'

'I won't be in.' I hesitated. 'Look, Constance, I know this is a lot to ask, but I've got to get over to the General Mercy Hospital over by the Bronx. Can you pick me up and take me there?'

'Emergency?'

'Perhaps; I don't know until I get there.'

'Ten minutes,' she said, and rang off.

It was seven and I was waiting by the door when she pulled into the kerb. The cold, pre-dawn air had started me shivering again, and I was glad of the bottle she seemed to carry as an accessory to her car. She didn't speak during the drive and I didn't try any smart conversation either.

She followed me into the hospital and stood by while I asked the necessary questions and found the right people. The intern who had called me was a fresh-faced youngster who had already seen enough of life to get cynical and not seen enough to get sympathetic. That would come later. He smiled at Constance, looked at me, then smiled at Constance again.

I couldn't blame him, but I was in a hurry.

'Where is he?'

'In the casualty ward. We're operating within the

hour.'

'Take me to him.'

'Well,' he hesitated. 'Unless it's essential I'd rather not wake him. I—'

'It's a case of murder,' I snapped. 'Take me to him.'

* * * * * * *

It was Pug all right. He lay, swathed in bandages and looking like a mummy. He was breathing, I could tell that from the sounds he was making, but that's about all I could tell. I stepped to his side.

'Pug.'

No answer.

'Pug, you lame-brain. It's me, Mike, open up that yap of yours and spill it.'

Crude? Maybe, but I was speaking his language and he needed the boost. He stirred, opened his eyes, and grinned at me.

'Hi, Mike.'

'You saw him? The killer?'

He nodded. He knew what I was talking about, so his mind wasn't affected, but his injuries had done something to his time sense. He grinned again.

'Spill it,' I urged. 'What happened?'

He thought about it. He thought about it while a nurse fussed at my side and the intern looked grave. Constance didn't say anything and, aside from the little sounds made by Pug's breathing, the ward was like a morgue.

'I was there, Mike. I didn't let you down.'

'I know that, Pug. What happened?'

'He came. I was waiting for him.' He breathed and I tried not to think of the pain he was in. 'I went out, you know, and heard the shot. I came back just in time to hear someone rushing down the stairs. I followed him.'

'The killer.' I nodded. 'Go on, Pug. What happened then?'

'Lost him in the snow. Looked for him. He must have had a car because he came at me. Knocked me down.' Pug swallowed again and I could see the beads of sweat on his face. 'Lousy driver, missed and stopped. I tried to swing at him and he sapped me. That's all.'

'Who was he, Pug? Describe him!'

'I—' Pug swallowed again. 'He—'

'That's enough.' The intern stepped forward and nodded to the nurse. Before I could say anything she had stuck a hypodermic into Pug's arm and I knew that more words would be a waste of time. I touched my face and was surprised to find that I was sweating.

'Will he live?'

'I think so.' The intern was professionally cheerful as he ushered us out. 'From what I can tell he was knocked down, sapped, and then run over. A man found him lying in a gutter and called the police. They passed him over to us.'

I looked around. I couldn't see anything that looked like a policeman.

'I told him to come back later,' explained the intern. 'Nothing he could do here anyway.'

'No,' I said bitterly. 'Nothing but sit beside him and

wait for him to talk. Or maybe they just don't want to know about it?'

'Maybe I didn't want him bothered,' said the intern and I looked at him with a new respect. Young, yes. Brash, yes. Dumb, no. He'd probably had the police in his hair before, and thought more of saving a life than that some rookie should fill his notebook with dying mumbles. I grinned at him.

'Sorry, and thanks for calling me. Do your best for him, Doc.'

'We always do that.'

'I know, but you know what I mean. The sky's the limit, send the bills to me.'

He nodded and somehow I got the impression that he didn't like me anymore. I didn't blame him.

'I'm a friend of his,' I said quietly. 'Does that explain anything?'

'Yes,' he said and smiled. 'Sorry, but it always gets under my skin when people think we only do our best work for money.'

'Forget it. When will he be able to talk?'

'After he comes out of the anaesthetic.'

'Not so good. Try again, Doc. Remember, I don't want him worried.'

'Two days, if you mean what I think you mean. Do you?'

'He didn't see the man who ran him down. He didn't see the actual face of the murderer. I believe that but the police wouldn't. They won't give him a minute's rest and, as soon as he can walk, they'll drag him down for questioning. I want him to get well, Doc. Give him a few hours to sort himself out and he'll know what to do. Spring the cops on him while he's groggy and he'll talk himself into jail.'

'I understand,' he said.

I hoped that he did.

Constance remained silent until we entered her car and then she asked me:

'What's it all about, Mike?'

'A man, Harmond, was shot in my office a while ago. Pug was supposed to be with him. He'd stepped out for a minute and while he was away the killer pulled the trigger. Pug came back and chased him. He got sapped and run over for his trouble, but even at that he was lucky. If he'd stayed in the office with Harmond he'd have been shot too.'

'Or he might have saved Harmond,' she said quietly.

I shook my head. 'No. That guy is playing for keeps. Pug would have just been another target.'

She sat silent for so long that I felt I had to say something.

'What's on your mind, Constance?'

'You know how it would look to the police if they wanted it to look that way?'

'Sure. I arranged for Harmond to be at my office and for Pug to kill him. Then, to get rid of Pug, I sapped him and staged an accident. I thought of that, that's why I want to keep the police out of his hair.' I stared at her. 'What do you think?'

'I think you're crazy,' she said. 'But I don't think

that you're a killer. Under wraps?'

'I can't ask that,' I said. 'If you want to use what you've got, then use it.'

'But if I don't?'

'I'll hand you the scoop on a platter—unless I get my head beaten off first.'

'I'd rather you kept your health,' she said, and didn't say another word all the way back to where I lived.

I found the apartment as I'd left it. I stared one more time at the pawn ticket and the receipts, then I peeled off my clothes, took a drink to keep the cold out, and fell into bed.

Sleep hit me like a ton of bricks.

CHAPTER TEN

I awoke at two in the afternoon, shivering with cold and with a mouth which seemed to be lined with fur. Crawling from my bed, I knocked over the bottle of Scotch and took a quick drink. It stayed down, so I took another, the spirit both warming me and cutting some of the slime from around my teeth. A shower, a shave, and a pot of coffee restored me halfway to normal.

I went through the usual routine of dressing, not forgetting to check my gun before tucking it under my arm, and then ventured out into the cold. I dropped past the bank and drew out some spending money. I ate a quick meal and had some more coffee, then I dropped into police headquarters and asked to see Captain Bresholm.

He nodded at me as I entered his office. His eyes were heavy with lack of sleep and his chin dark with stubble. He yawned and pushed a sheaf of typed sheets towards me.

'Your statement. Sign three copies.'

I signed three copies.

'You look like hell,' said Bresholm cheerfully. He

lit a cigar and I wondered at the state of his stomach. I refused his offer of one and gave myself a cigarette.

'Anything new?'

'He was killed with a slug from a point-thirty-eight automatic. Death was instantaneous.' He yawned again. 'The usual thing. The Doc sets the time of death around nine-thirty which, incidentally, doesn't let you out as a suspect.'

'We've been through all that,' I said. 'Get anything from his stuff?'

'This?' Bresholm took a fat envelope from his drawer and spilled out the contents of Harmon's pockets. 'Not a thing. The photograph is as old as you'd think it is, some girl he knew when he was young, I expect. We've checked his room at the big house with the same result. Nothing.'

'Enemies?'

'None, not as far as we can tell, but there must be at least one, mustn't there?'

'That or someone thought he knew too much and wanted to stop him talking.'

'I've thought of that,' he said seriously. 'It adds up, doesn't it? Any idea as to what he was going to tell you?'

'No.'

'I didn't think you had.' He shoved the stuff back into the envelope and put it away. He rubbed his chin and ran his tongue around the inside of his mouth. He looked all in.

'How about the kids?'

'Stephan was drunk, as usual. Susan didn't get home until around dawn. She was escorted and her alibi is better than yours. No soap.'

'The staff?'

'The maid went out, she says to a movie, we're checking on that now. The chauffeur, Marvin, he was around until past midnight when he took a drive. He's clear. '

'The Colonel?'

'Suspicious, aren't you? He was at one of his clubs until well after the shooting. Try again.'

'I can't. I've run out of suspects.' I breathed smoke towards him. 'What gives with Thornedyke?'

'Thornedyke?' A veil seemed to drop before Bresholm's eyes.

'You know who I mean. The smart operator out at the Purple Orchid. Well?'

'A gambler. Running his place against the law, but who cares about that.' Bresholm sucked his teeth. 'At least, that's what people keep telling me. I'm Homicide, remember, not the vice squad.'

'Protection?'

'I wouldn't know.' He smiled blandly, enigmatically, and I knew it was time for me to change the subject.

Gambling, when you came down to it, wasn't so bad. Not as bad as dope and the reefer racket. But it was still against the law. Officially, Thornedyke couldn't exist, but the fact that he did meant that someone was pulling down some heavy sugar. For a decent cop it wasn't something to be proud of.

Bresholm was a decent cop.

I got up and said goodbye and promised to let him know if anything happened. Outside I sniffed at the cold air and then caught a cab. It dropped me outside a pawn shop, and I went in and showed the man behind the counter the ticket I had taken from Harmond.

He was a smooth-faced character who saw a lot more than he ever let on about, and his eyes, as they searched my face, were as wise as time. He fingered the pasteboard.

'Your pledge?'

'Does it matter?'

'Not if you have the ticket,' he admitted. 'You want to redeem it?'

'That's the idea.' I dug money from my pocket and passed it to him. He counted it, rang it up on a cash register, and was about to take the ticket when I stopped him. 'Leave it.'

He stared at me, then shrugged. He glanced at the number, went somewhere, and came back with a ladies' wristwatch. It wasn't what I'd expected.

'Is this it?'

'Yes.'

I took it, turning it over in my hands. It was old, wellworn, an inexpensive sort of watch, the kind a couple of loving parents would give to their daughter when she reached the age when she started thinking about dates and boyfriends and getting married. It had stopped and I gave the stem a couple of turns. The ticking sounded like the works of a time-bomb.

I turned it over and stared at the back.

There was an inscription on it. Faded now and almost worn away with time and friction, but, holding it against the light, I could make out what it said.

A name, Rhoda Fleming. A date, a town, and words to the effect that it had been given by a Mr. and Mrs. Fleming to their daughter on her sixteenth birthday.

There was also a pawnbroker's mark, the only one, and I looked at the man behind the counter.

'This your mark?'

'Yes.' He leaned forward and took the watch from my hand. 'Look, mister,' he said quietly. 'You know your own business, but I'd say that this watch isn't yours.'

'You'd be right,' I agreed. 'It isn't. I'm redeeming it for a friend.' I looked at him. 'An old guy, looks like a butler, name of Harmond. Recognise him?'

'No.'

'How long ago was this watch pledged?'

'Don't you know?'

I thumbed out one of my cards and dropped it on to the counter.

'I'm a private eye on a case. I don't want anything from you but a couple of answers. You needn't give them to me if you don't want to, but maybe you'd rather give them to me than to the police.'

I gave him time to think about it.

'How long ago? A week? Two weeks?'

'Ten days, the date's on the ticket.'

I wondered what was wrong with me that I hadn't

already thought of that.

'Did I describe the man who pledged it?'

'Near enough. Look, mister, what's all this about?'

'Nothing that could trouble you.' I held out my hand for the watch and he gave it to me. I read the inscription again then pushed it back towards him. 'Right. Take it back and let me have the ticket.'

'You're repledging it?'

'Not exactly. Let's just say that I haven't been in here at all.' I winked at him. 'Understand?'

'No.' He went across to the cash register and rang it open. He took out my money and threw it down in front of me. I picked it up, peeled off a five-dollar bill and, putting the rest away, left the fin on the counter.

It was still lying there when I walked out into the street. I had a couple of drinks at a bar, not because I wanted them, but because I felt cold, and wondered whether or not I was going to come down with pneumonia. While in the bar I remembered to call the agency to see if there were any messages for me. There were three, one from the Smith character, one from the hospital informing me that Pug had been operated on and was on the road back to health, and one from a man named Jelkson who wanted me to ring him back.

I rang him back.

'Mr. Lantry?' The voice was smooth with the tiredness of age. Not a cultured voice, not a harsh, too-smart voice, just the voice of a decent man who was getting tired of trying to make ends meet.

'That's right. You wanted me?'

'I've got something which belongs to you, a wallet. Is it yours?'

'Could be.'

'It's got your card in it, and a shield, and a licence and some other stuff. Would you like to collect it?'

'I'm busy right now,' I said. 'Could you fetch it to me, you have my address?' I sensed his hesitation. 'I'll make it worth your while. Can you?'

'In an hour,' he said. 'Will that be all right with you?'

'Fine,' I said. 'Just fine.'

From the bar I went to a post office where I sent off ten dollars to Fred and the fifty I owed to Smith. I like to settle my debts while I'm still alive. I didn't owe Smith fifty, but the extra ten was for having kept him waiting, and I thought that he'd earned it. From the post office I dropped off at the *Tribune* building, smiled at the sour-faced receptionist, and asked for admittance to the morgue.

This time she didn't argue.

Harry blinked at me when I told him what I wanted.

'Hard to tell,' he said. 'If she was in the news, yes. If not, no. It'll take a little time.'

'How much time?' I glanced at my watch. 'Couple of hours?'

'At least. I'll have to contact the wire services and scout around. This business or private?'

'It could be both.' I grinned at him. 'You know me?'

'Sure I know you, why?'

'Nothing. You want fifty?'

'Who doesn't,' he said, and grinned back. 'Okay, I'll

get on to it.'

I left it at that.

Jelkson was a thin, dried-up little man with a head too big for his shoulders and a worried expression. He was waiting outside the office when I arrived and began to speak as soon as I opened the door.

'It's this way, Mr. Lantry. I found this wallet and took a look inside. I saw your card and thought that maybe you'd want it back.'

'You thought right.' I held out my hand. 'Give.'

He gave.

I checked the wallet. My licence, the badge, some cards, the usual stuff. No money. I looked at him.

'It was clean when I found it,' he said unhappily. 'I hope that you don't think I'd take any money if it was there?'

'I know it wasn't there,' I said. I looked at him. 'Why didn't you post it?'

He wriggled at that one and I could tell the answer from the expression in his eyes. He was decent all right, and he didn't like what he was doing, but sometimes a man has to take what he can. I reached for my pocket and took out some money.

'So you want to be paid. How much?'

'I—' He swallowed again. 'I thought—' He gave it up. I was deliberately curt.

'Come on, man. You want it, ask for it, how much?'

'Nothing,' he said, and with the refusal he seemed to recover his lost dignity. 'Take it as a favour.'

'No,' I said, and waved for him to sit down. 'Married?'

'Yes.'

'Kids?'

'Three.'

'Wife sick?'

'How did you know?'

I didn't bother to tell him. I've been around and I can recognise the signs when I see them. Shabby clothing, a summer overcoat in winter weather, the too-big eyes, and the waxen skin. The guy was starving himself and it was easy to guess why. I hefted the wallet.

'This, in itself, isn't very valuable,' I told him. 'You saved me the inconvenience of having to get a duplicate licence and badge, but that's about all. Where did you find it?'

'In a trash can. Sam's pool rooms, down on the East Side.'

I nodded, not asking him what he was doing prowling around trash cans, but he told me just the same.

'I'm a garbage collector,' he said. 'On that job you get used to sorting the trash in case there's anything of value. You'd be surprised at some of the things we find.' He flushed. 'Don't think that I'm a crook or anything like that, but the city pay's pretty low wages and—'

'I understand. So you try to make a little on the side.' I nodded. 'So you found this leather dumped in a trash can belonging to Sam's pool rooms. Give me the address.'

He gave me the address.

'Does anyone else know about this?'

'No,' he said, and flushed again. For a garbage

collector he was quite a sensitive guy.

'Good.' I reached for my money. 'The cost of replacing the stuff in the wallet would be about ten dollars.' I gave him ten dollars. 'The wallet itself another five.' I gave him five more. 'And the information as to where you got it and for buttoning your lip now and forever is worth the balance of fifty.' I counted out more money and pushed the half-century towards him. 'Okay?'

'Gee, thanks, Mr. Lantry.' He hesitated, one hand almost touching the money. 'You don't have to do this, you know. I was hoping for maybe a dollar for my trouble, but this is too much.'

'Not to me it isn't.' I flicked him one of my cards. 'If ever you're in trouble, or if ever you think you can help me in some way, let me know. If the information is worth anything, I'll pay you. Fair enough?'

He nodded, his Adam's apple bobbing in his throat, and I guessed that he'd already decided how to spend the money.

I hoped that he'd treat himself to a new coat but, knowing his type, I guessed that himself would be the last thing he'd think about.

I stood at the window watching him scuttle down the street. It was getting dark again, and more snow was on the way. I sighed as I stared after him. In my business you meet all kinds, and you have to meet all kinds to stay in business. Some try to use you, others you can use, but I tried not to make enemies unless I chose them.

A garbage collector wasn't much, but he was two eyes and two ears and a mouth. He got around. He was grateful to me and, if he heard anything, he'd let me know. Little things? Sure, but that's the way big agencies are made.

I intended to get a big agency one day.

If I lived long enough.

The phone jarred and I answered it. It was Constance, trying the office before leaving word at the agency or maybe she wouldn't have left word anyway.

'Mike, you chiseller. What gives with Harry?'

'He told you?'

'Some, not all. What are you after?'

'A hunch.'

'In Texas? Who are you trying to kid?'

'No one.' I grinned into the phone at her snort of disbelief. 'Look, Constance, we've an agreement. Play it my way and you won't lose on it. Gum it up and neither of us gets anywhere. Did Harry get it yet?'

'Give him time.' She became thoughtful. 'Rhoda Fleming, have I heard that name somewhere?'

'I doubt it.'

'You're a close-mouthed operator, Mike. I don't get you. Built like a bruiser and with the face of a battered saint.

What are you trying to do now? Find a murderer?'

'Maybe.'

'This way?'

'Maybe.'

'Don't want to talk, eh?' She chuckled. 'Okay, Mike, I won't jam the works. I'll expect to hear from you though.'

'You'll hear from me,' I promised, and hung up. I looked at the phone then, on impulse, I dialled a number.

'Yes, sir?'

The voice was smooth, polite, too polite, the voice of a heel.

'Is that the Purple Orchid?'

'Yes, sir.'

'I'd like to speak to one of your young ladies. I met her the other night, Georgette her name is; will you connect me please.'

'I'm sorry, sir,' the voice remained smooth, but now there was the hint of a bite in it. 'Our hostesses are not allowed to receive personal messages.'

'No? Well give me her home number then and I'll contact her myself.'

'We are not allowed to do that.'

'No? What sort of a crummy joint is that? Put me on to the boss and I'll ask him myself.'

'I'll try, sir, who is speaking, please?'

'John Weston,' I said. 'Look, forget the boss, just tell Georgette that her friend, the one she met last night and who offered her a nice vacation, wants to see her. Will you do that?'

'Well—' The voice struggled to remain polite. 'I'm not sure that—'

'Skip it!' I thickened my voice to a growl. 'Save the syrup for the suckers. Give the dame my message, she'll understand, and I'll expect her to phone me. If I don't hear from her, I'm coming up there, and if you haven't given her the message I'll rip your ears off. Get it?'

'A tough guy, uh?' Now the voice was no longer polite. No matter how you dress a heel, he's still a heel. Rub him the wrong way and his true nature sticks out a mile. I grinned into the phone.

'Tough enough to take you, fellow,' I growled. 'You and that fancy layout upstairs. Do as I say or I'll see what a little persuasion will do. Now get the lead out of your pants and tell the dame she's wanted.'

'She ain't here,' the voice snarled. 'It's early yet.'

'Okay. Then pass her the word, or else!'

I hung up before he could break my eardrum.

I sat for a while staring at the phone, but not really expecting an answer. Maybe they would tell Georgette, or maybe they wouldn't. Thornedyke must have had plenty of experience in handling the would-be tough boys who had a big mouth and nothing else. Still, they might ask her who John Weston was supposed to be and, if she had any sense at all, she might guess who had called. I hoped so.

After a while I rose and checked the Browning. I tucked my money into my newly recovered wallet, and put the wallet into my pocket. I took a last look around the office, made sure that the bottom drawer was really empty of Scotch, and went out into the corridor.

I didn't send for the elevator, I wanted to try Bresholm's theory, and I felt a little sorry for the old janitor.

So I let him sleep as I stepped out of the building. I

wasn't in a hurry anyway.

I was going to play some pool.

CHAPTER ELEVEN

Sam's pool rooms consisted of a couple of plate-glass windows, a swing-door, and an uneven floor on which stood a dozen tables. A bar to one side sold hot-dogs, coffee, candy bars, and similar junk. A man leaned behind the counter, with a wooden board close to him against one wall on which he kept the tabs of those who were playing. A marker, a broken-down jockey by the look of him, shuffled about and kept the cues in order.

On the surface the pool room looked like any one of a thousand others, a place to play pool, billiards, or even a little crap if no one was looking, but I knew that I only saw the half of it.

There was a back room where they would have a line to the race track. There were other rooms where hard liquor was sold and private poker games held. It was a collecting point for the numbers game and similar rackets. It was the hang-out of adolescent heels, muggers, and heist boys, a place where you could buy a gunsel to kill a man, a couple of toughs to beat up someone you didn't like, the sort of dive where youngsters took their first steps towards the electric chair.

I let the doors swing behind me and looked the place over. The few men in the place looked me over too, halting their play while they watched me from the shadow of hat brims, their eyes narrowed and sharp like those of the rats they resembled. I walked over to the counter and bought a thick mug of slimy coffee. I sipped it, spat, and glared at the counter-man.

'What's the matter with this dump? No liquor?'

'Not allowed to sell it.' He peered at me from scarred eyes obviously trying to place me. 'Fresh in town?'

'Maybe.' I fumbled out a cigarette and blew smoke towards him. 'Seen Lefty?'

'Who?'

'Or Spike?'

'Never heard of them.'

'No?' I shrugged. 'Too bad. They told me to look them up whenever I hit town. Anything going on in the back room?'

He didn't answer that one and I didn't expect him to. I jerked a thumb towards the tables.

'Book me up.'

'That'll be fifty cents,' he said, not moving. I threw him a dollar.

'Let me know if Lefty or Spike comes in,' I said. 'I'll be catching up on my pool.'

I found a partner, some slant-eyed youngster who could have made a fortune playing in competitions if he hadn't thought it smarter to hang around the fringe of the underworld. He let me win the fall-game, and then upped the ante for the next. I won that too, which surprised him, and agreed to play for double or quits. He won, easily but not by too big a margin, and looked at me as he chalked his cue.

'Make this a real one?'

'Why not?'

'A sawbuck?'

'I thought you said make it a real one?' I squinted at him through the smoke of my cigarette. 'A grand?'

He hesitated. He could win and he knew it, but he didn't know me. He decided to take a chance.

'Sure, if you say so.' I stopped him as he was about to break.

'Hold it, pal. You got that kind of money?'

'Sure.' He tried to bluster and I knew that he was lying. I changed my voice for a growl.

'Listen, sonny! If you play with me, you've got the moola to pay if you lose or else. Get me?'

'Sure,' he said, and his eyes scurried around in his head like a couple of white mice. 'I ain't no welcher.'

'No? Then show the coin.'

I watched him while he sweated.

'Okay. We'll make it a sawbuck,' I said. 'I ain't got no time to argue.'

He was so rattled he lost hands down.

I tucked the greasy bill into my pocket and licked my lips.

'Hell, ain't there no place where we can get a snort around here? Lefty told me this was a right joint.'

'Lefty?'

'Yeah. You know him?'

'Some.' The guy, like all of his breed, was eager to bask in reflected glory. He glanced over his shoulder and lowered his voice. 'I might be able to fix an "in" for you. You look a right guy and this is a right place. Where you from?'

'Leavenworth,' I said and didn't smile as I mentioned the prison. 'Don't play patsy with me. Lefty knows me, Spike too; if there's an "in" I want it.' I took out his ten-dollar bill, screwed it into a ball, and tossed it towards him. 'Here, buy yourself a candy bar.'

He glared at me as he stooped for the bill. He didn't like me and yet he envied me. Guys like that always envy a man who acts big and talks big and has money to flash around. He lowered his voice and sidled up to me.

'Wait around a while. If I get you in, what's it worth?'

'A century.' I turned away from him and began hitting balls across the table. I concentrated on some tricky shots and was just getting my hand in when I felt someone standing behind me. I turned, slowly, and stared at him.

'Hello, shamus.'

The purr was the same, the big hand with the big ring was the same, the mad, animal-gleam in the eyes. I looked at him, then glanced around. We were alone, the others had sensed something was up and had vanished. Even the marker was out of sight, probably behind the counter. Only the ex-fighter who ran the joint was visible. He walked towards us, a short club swinging from one hand.

'Take it easy, Lefty.'

'I thought that you didn't know him?' I said.

'Button your lip, wise guy.' He didn't look at me and I could see little beads of sweat on his upper lip. He stared hard at the gunsel. 'You heard what I said, Lefty?'

'I heard you, Sam.'

'Lefty is hot,' I said calmly. 'He's liable to cut loose at any moment, aren't you, Lefty?'

'That's right, shamus.'

'See.' I flicked my eyes towards Sam. 'He runs the joint, not you. Right, Lefty?'

'Right, shamus.'

'Where's Spike?'

'Waiting for you.' He grinned, showing me his blackened teeth. 'He's all cosy in the back room. Come and join us, copper!'

'That'll be lovely,' I said. 'Music too?'

'Maybe.' Lefty drew his hand from his pocket and I saw something in his hand. He pressed a switch and five inches of steel flashed out towards me. I tensed and he grinned as he looked down at the switch-knife.

'Neat,' I said. 'Where did you get it?'

'Out of a Christmas cracker.' He gestured with the blade. 'Come on, shamus. Nice and easy now; you wouldn't like to get this in your kidney now, would you?'

I got the point.

So did Sam.

He stepped forward, the club poised in one big hand,

and his eyes looked scared.

'I've told you before, Lefty,' he gritted. 'No rough stuff in here. Take him outside if you want to beat him up, but not in here.'

'Pipe down,' said Lefty.

'I've told you—'

Lefty hardly seemed to move but suddenly Sam squealed and stared down at his shirt front. It was slit from side to side as neatly as though done with a pair of scissors. Lefty grinned.

'Button your lip, Sam, and go peddle your coffee. I'll take care of the shamus.' His purr deepened as he looked at me. 'I'll take care of him but good.'

Spike was sitting at a small table nursing a bottle of Scotch when we entered. Lefty was taking his time, enjoying every moment of it, and I could see that Spike didn't like what was going on a bit. He was scared of Lefty, yet he didn't have the guts to break loose from the big man's dominance. He gulped Scotch and tried to make out he wasn't there.

Lefty chuckled and prodded me with the tip of the knife.

'Okay, shamus, start something.'

I did.

I took a step forward and sent my left hand, the one holding the billiard ball I'd just picked off the table, swinging towards his face. I let the ball go at just the right moment and it smashed against the bridge of his nose with a satisfying thud. He squealed, his hands flying up to his ruined nose, the knife falling to stick point-down in the floor.

Then I concentrated on Spike.

He was trying to do three things at once, and making a poor job of each of them. He was trying to get up, to draw a gun, and to hit me with the bottle. I ducked the bottle, shoved forward against the table, and, by the time he had realised what was happening, I'd half-shoved the muzzle of my gun down his throat.

He looked up at me with eyes as scared as those of a rabbit who sees a snake.

'Relax,' I said, and felt under his arm. He had a gun all right, a Browning, *my* Browning, and I slipped it into my jacket pocket. Something groaned behind me, and I turned in time to watch Lefty crawl across the floor towards his knife. I laid the side of my gun against his temple, picked up the knife, relieved him of the weight of a .45 revolver, and looked at Spike again.

'Well?'

'Don't hit me, mister,' he whined. 'It wasn't me, honest it wasn't. It was Lefty who sapped you and dumped you out to freeze.'

'Was it?' I slapped him, lightly, and dragged him upright. I straightened the chair and put him on it. I found another and collected the bottle. It hadn't broken and it was good Scotch. I tried some.

Spike watched me, his eyes getting more and more scared. Lefty didn't watch me, he breathed through his mouth and rested. I wasted no time on Lefty.

'Who employed you to give me the works?'

'I don't know, mister. Honest I don't!'

I slapped him again, not so lightly, and repeated the question.

'We got a phone call,' he babbled. 'At least, Lefty did. I just went along for the ride.'

'And the dough?'

'Lefty took it.'

'Get it.'

I waited while Spike lifted a wallet from the sleeping man's pocket and took out a wad of bills. I took them from his shaking fingers, counted out what was due to me, then flung the rest on the floor. Stupid? Maybe, but his money I could do without.

'Listen, Spike,' I said grimly. 'You took me for a ride, beat me up, left me to freeze or worse. Someone paid you to do it. Who?'

'I don't know, mister. I'd tell you if I did.'

I believed him. Spike was a parasite, hanging on to a tough guy because he was too timid to operate on his own. I'd knocked out the wrong man.

I looked down at Lefty, still breathing, still lying in his own blood. I'd broken his nose, I'd bruised his temple and his stomach. I'd shaken loose a few teeth, but it wasn't enough. I should have killed him while I was at it, his sort are better off dead.

'Listen,' I said. 'Tell Lefty, when he recovers, that if he's got any bright ideas about me to forget them. The next time we tangle, I'll tie his arms in knots and throw him in the river.' I took another drink. 'The same goes for you too. Turn around.'

'What?'

'You heard me, turn around.'

He didn't like doing it. He thought he knew what was going to happen, but he was wrong. I didn't sap him. Instead I left him staring at the wall, trembling, wet with his own sweat, terrified of what he had so often done to others.

I left him like that.

In the big room outside, the players had gathered around the tables again. Sam, the owner, rested thick arms on his counter and looked worried. I nodded to him, grinning at his expression, and got away from there as fast as I could.

I felt as if I needed a bath.

CHAPTER TWELVE

354 Green Street was a relic of the days when the area had been decent, a long time ago now. A tall, brownstone building with rotting walls and a sewer smell wafting through the rotting front door. I stared at the row of bells, found the one which belonged to Mr. Jenkin, and pressed the second one above it. I waited for maybe ten seconds, pressed it again and, after another long wait, shoved my thumb hard against the one below.

This time the door-latch clicked like a petulant hen, and I pushed open the door before the person upstairs could wonder who was calling. Inside, the dirt and sewer smell made me gag, but I held on and climbed up the grimy staircase.

Sam Jenkin's apartment was on the sixth floor. A shadowed doorway set back off the staircase, bearing a small white card which looked at me like an accusing eye. Above me, on the next floor, a door slammed and a woman's voice, thin and peevish, called down the stairs.

'Who is it?'

I didn't answer.

'Who wants me?'

I still didn't answer and, after a while, she slammed the door again, muttering something beneath her breath.

After I was sure that she had gone, I turned my attention to the apartment. Gently I tried the door; it was locked, so I rested my ear against the panel and thumbed the doorbell. I could hear it ringing from somewhere inside but that was all I could hear. I tried again, same result. Mr. Jenkin was either out or didn't live there anymore.

From my wallet I slipped the thick piece of transparent celluloid I use to keep the front of my licence clean and, leaning heavily against the door, I shoved it hard between the door-edge and the jamb. I hit something, pressed harder, and the door swung open.

I put the celluloid back where it belonged, slipped the Browning from beneath my arm and, holding it against my ribs, entered the apartment.

Nothing happened.

No shots, no screams, no yells for help. Nothing. I shut the door and rested my back against the wall as I let my eyes drift over what I could see. After a while I put the gun away and began to move around a little. Still nothing. I was alone. I switched on the light.

The apartment was one of those conversions with a bed-sitting room, kitchen, and bath. The bed-sitting room had a folding bed disguised as an inlaid panel, but it was still a bed. I stood in the middle of the room and had a look round.

It wasn't a nice sight.

It was dusty. It was dirty. It was cluttered with empty bottles, cigarette butts, and discarded newspapers. The kitchen looked as if it hadn't been used for the past three months, and the bathroom didn't appear to have been used at all. I stepped through the kitchen and squinted down the rusty fire-escape. I went back into the main room and found a chair, and sat in it while I smoked a cigarette.

I smoked slowly and thoughtfully and stared around the compact room. An inset wardrobe stood in one corner looking like a vertical coffin. A chest of drawers, a bedside table, a regular table, two chairs, a couple of glasses, and that was about all. I rose and stepped towards the chest of drawers. It wasn't even locked and I examined it, looking for I don't know what.

All I found was an unopened bottle of rye.

I found a glass and washed it clean. I opened the rye and took a drink. I smoked and took another drink. I looked at the phone standing on the bedside table, glanced at my watch, and decided to wait a little longer. What I was waiting for I didn't know, but something, some sort of a hunch, kept me glued to the apartment.

I killed two cigarettes and half the bottle and then I got up and slipped the gun from under my arm. I crossed to the wardrobe and jerked it open. Nothing. No clothes, no hangers, not even a mothball. I checked the bathroom again, the kitchen, then turned back to the main room. Slowly I approached the bed. It was a simple thing, the usual type. A double bed hinged at the head and swung up into a recess in the wall so that it would be out of the way during the day. A simple catch held it upright.

I reached for the catch.

The bed almost hit me as it swung down, the folding legs slamming against the floor as if they wanted to go through it. As it fell my nose crinkled to a wave of perfume, expensive perfume, and then I knew what had made me linger in the apartment. With the perfume came a different smell, acrid, unpleasant, and I filled my lungs with cigarette smoke letting it trickle through my nostrils as I leaned forward and stared down at the bed.

I looked at ten thousand dollars.

She lay, her head towards the headrest, her hair streaming over the rumpled pillows, her contorted features bearing little resemblance to the photograph I had in my pocket. Her costume, brown tweed, was creased. Her fur coat was a twisted mess and one of her shoes had slipped from her foot. Her fingernails were broken and her throat bore deep scratches.

She was very dead.

I sniffed again, separating the odours of death and perfume from other, ranker odours. I picked up one arm and let it fall limply back to the bed. Then I lit a fresh cigarette, took a swig of rye, and set to work.

It was a waste of time.

Neither bed nor body yielded the slightest clue, and I stood, looking down at her, mentally apologising for having disturbed her final rest. She stared back at me, her mouth half open, her eyes glazed, but she didn't care.

The dead never care.

The jangling of the phone made me start and twist like a shocked animal, the Browning leaping as if of itself into my hand, my lips aching from where they had drawn back hard against my teeth. I stood there, glaring at the instrument, letting my heart slow and my breath return. My hand ached from the force with which I held the gun and I stared at it, wondering what it was doing in my hand.

The phone rang again and again and kept on ringing. It sounded long enough to wake the dead, but it didn't quite do that. After what seemed a couple of eternities it stopped, and I began to breathe again.

I put the gun away, gripped hold of the end of the bed, and swung it back into position. I took out my handkerchief and went around wiping wherever I had touched. Once I turned sharply to look towards the bed, but the catch had held and I knew that she couldn't make a sound. The apartment seemed normal. Nice and dirty and unlived in.

I took another drink, washed the glass, wiped the bottle and remembered to polish the light switch. Then, after a last look round, I eased open the door, took a peep outside, and stepped into the hall letting the door swing shut behind me.

I headed for the stairs.

I almost made it, I was a single flight from the door when I heard voices from outside and it swung open.

A man walked in accompanied by a woman and, as I moved, they stared at me. I raised my hat.

'Good-evening.'

I kept the hat between my face and theirs until I was outside. Polite? Maybe, but I didn't want anyone to recognise me if they should be asked. Not that I was in much danger of that. Green Street was the sort of neighbourhood where everyone minds their own business, and can't remember the time if a cop should ask them.

My watch warned me that it was getting late and I hurried through the slush back towards civilisation. Around me tall buildings made the night darker than what it was. Rats lived in those buildings, human rats with sharp eyes and itchy fingers. They lurked in darkness and dirt, spinning their little webs always after the easy dollar, and leaving a trail of their own slime as a snail marks its own passage.

I was glad to catch a cab out of it.

I stopped off at a tavern and phoned the agency. I gave my code number and the mechanical voice told me that there was one message for me. A name and a phone number. Georgette's name. I fed coins into the slot and dialled.

'Hello?'

'That Georgette?'

'Yes. Who's that?'

'Lantry. You've got something for me?'

'Maybe.' Her voice sounded thick as though she'd been crying. 'You on the up and up about that deal?'

'Sure.' Norma was dead but I didn't have to tell her that. 'What you got for sale?'

'Listen. Thornedyke's sore at you. You know that?'

'I had an idea. Why?'

'He used to be sweet on Norma and doesn't like you asking questions.'

'So I've gathered. That's not news, Georgette, not saleable news anyway.'

'No,' she said, and paused. 'Look, I might be a heel telling you this, but what the hell, a girl's got to live hasn't she?'

'You should know.'

'I do, shamus, listen. Norma's a good kid, none better, but we all make mistakes and sometimes we never finish paying for them. I don't want to cause her any grief, but I think she might be in trouble. She—'
There was the sound of an indrawn breath and a man's voice muffled as though it came through a door.

'Hello?'

'Skip it, call you later.'

'Wait!'

'No soap, leave it.'

'I'll call you back. Same number, when?'

'Anytime, dearies,' she crooned and now the man's voice was loud as though he had entered the room. 'Look, I've got an awful headache and I'm taking a rest. Call me and let me know whether you got him to propose or not. Play it smart, dearie, and you'll have diamonds on both hands at the same time. Need any help, just call on me, I've had experience.'

She chuckled and hung up.
I went in search of something to eat.

CHAPTER THIRTEEN

After getting outside a thick steak and a heap of French-fries, I dropped in at the *Tribune* building. Harry was waiting for me, his pale face thoughtful.

'Get it?'

'I got something.' He handed me a couple of files and I took them over to the desk. Constance joined me as I was searching through them.

'Well?'

'Not so well.' I pointed to the files. 'What's the matter, the organisation break down?'

'You asked too much.' She picked up a teletyped slip and read the code most newspaper men use among themselves. It saves time, money, and tells a lot in a short space. 'Nothing at the wire service, nothing at the agencies, and no news-pics. Your Rhoda Fleming must have been a shy girl.'

'In show business?' I shook my head.

'Sure this is all there is?'

'It's all we've got,' said Constance. 'This is unofficial, remember? And the services can't worry about every showgirl who kicks a leg in a third-rate dive. She'd only have her pic on file if she was news.'

'What about the other one then?'

'Mona Hartridge? Same thing.'

'What? No pictures of Mrs. Geeson?'

'Plenty of her, but none taken before she was married.' Constance riffled through the file. 'Correction One, but it's a bad print, you'd hardly recognise her for the same woman.'

I took the clipping from her hand and stared at it. It was a bad print, very bad, one with the head turned at an angle as if someone had just called her attention to something. As a likeness of Mrs. Geeson, it was terrible.

But as a likeness of someone else it wasn't too bad.

'Any good?' Constance took it, put it away, then stared at me with sudden suspicion. 'Mike! You've got something!'

'Have I?'

'You're darn right you have. I've seen that look before.' She made the age-old rubbing gesture with thumb and forefinger. 'Come on, spill it.'

'No.'

'Why not? Hell, Mike, you promised!'

'Look, Constance, I know that you newshooks have ink for blood, but just for once try and think of someone else.'

'The Colonel?' She was wiser than I thought. 'The kids? Give, Mike, I can be trusted.'

'I wonder?' I stared at her and read my answer in her eyes. 'Yes, you can be trusted. Sorry.'

'Skip it.' She smiled at me without embarrassment.

'Want to talk?'

'Off the record?'

'Way off. Well?'

I hesitated. It wasn't any of her business and yet, in a way, it was. Murder will out and Mrs. Geeson had been murdered. Nothing could save the Colonel from publicity now, but maybe a few friends in the right place to damp down the dirt would help a little.

I decided to take a chance.

'I'm dreaming,' I said. 'I'm making noises without sense, understand?'

'Shoot.'

'Take a girl, poor, hopeful, running herself ragged to make the big time. Take a boy, crazy about her and with an old man who's loaded. Take his mother, prim, proper, and who controls the finances. Add something else, what I don't know yet, stir, bring to the boil, and what do you get?'

'Trouble,' she said promptly.

I nodded. 'Trouble it is, but easy trouble, money trouble, the kind that can be fixed. Then suppose that the old woman dies, has an accident, and now the boy is crazy to get married. But the old man thinks a lot of his son, a hell of a lot. So he offers to marry her himself, buy her off, grab her before his son manages to talk her into taking a chance that he won't be cut off without the proverbial red cent. She falls for it. Why not? He's old, sure, but he's rich and she's wanted easy money all her life. Follow me so far?'

'Yes.' Constance frowned. 'Not pretty, is it?'

'Dirt never is. The kid went off the rails. Maybe she had some idea of taking the old man's dough and still run around with her stepson, but the boy was basically decent, he wouldn't play. Maybe the old man knew that. Maybe he did it all for the best, but it was a hell of a way to break things up. Or maybe I'm wrong. She could have been genuine. After all, the old man offered her a clean life, the sort she'd been wanting for a long time.'

I took time out to light a cigarette. Constance held out her hand and I passed one to her. She lit it from the tip of my own, her hair tickling my nose as she bent over. I wanted to kiss the nape of her neck but didn't.

'Then she ran out,' she said quietly 'Why?'

'I don't know. I can guess, but I'm not sure. I think that she didn't travel alone. She'd been around, was a good-looking girl, and may have picked up a husband on the way. You know how it is, sometimes it's easier to forget them than to get a divorce, and when she needed it, it was too late. She had to live the act out to the end.' I breathed smoke. 'The bitter end.'

'It adds up,' said Constance slowly. 'But where's the proof?'

'No proof.'

'But wouldn't the old man have checked?'

'He would. But how do you check a person? Paper proof, that's all anyone has.' I touched the clipping in the file. 'That isn't Mrs. Geeson. Now do you get it?'

'A switch!' She stared at me, the cigarette burning forgotten in her hand. 'But would it be possible?'

'Why not? You want to get married but you have a husband somewhere. You also have a friend who isn't and hasn't been married. You take her name, birthplace, identity. You marry under that name and with her birth certificate. Who's to know?'

'The friend?'

'Sure. But money can stop a mouth, and enough money can stop it for good. Or perhaps she didn't even know about the switch. This is a big country, Constance, and a lot of things can happen in it.'

She thought about it for a while, smoking, letting the smoke trickle from between her lips and coil around her head. She had a nicely shaped head. She shook it.

'No soap. You've forgotten something. The husband.'

I shrugged. 'I'm only guessing.'

'Unless—?' She shook her head. 'No. It's too dirty.'

'For ten million dollars a man will stand a lot of dirt,' I said. I glanced at my watch and levered myself off my chair. 'I've got to be moving. You on duty tonight?'

'No, but I could be.' She stared at me. 'Something due to break?'

'What gives you that idea?' I grinned at her and gave her the okay sign. 'I've got your number.'

'I'll be waiting. Photog?'

'He can keep you company,' I said. 'At home or here?'

'Here. I'll get in a poker session to occupy my mind.' She stepped towards me, put hands on my shoulders and stared into my eyes. She didn't have to tilt her head very far to do it either. 'I'll be waiting, Mike. Take care of yourself.'

'Don't bank on anything,' I warned. 'But keep your fingers crossed.'

She held them up to me as I pushed my way through the doors.

They were already crossed.

Outside the *Tribune* building I headed for a bar and a telephone. I collected some nickels and shut myself in a booth. I phoned Wendle. I had a lot of trouble getting him, but finally I unlevered him from a confab of his business partners and heard him snap as he took the phone:

'Yes? What is it?'

'Lantry here, Mr. Wendle. Who handles the payoff?'

He was no fool and cottoned on fast. I heard the sound of footsteps and the slamming of a door. Then he was back, breathing heavily into the receiver.

'You've found her?'

'Yes.' I let silence grow between us while he gave it some thought.

'Can I speak to her?'

'Not yet.' I stared into one of the little mirrors they put inside telephone booths and winked at my own reflection. 'She's kind of busy right now.'

'You mean that she's alive?'

'Of course, why not?' I winked at myself again. 'When can I collect?'

He didn't like that one, lawyers never do. He hedged.

'Surely that would be up to the Colonel. He hired you, not I.'

'That's right. I'd forgotten. Sorry.'

'Not at all.' He hesitated. 'Where will you be if I want to find you?'

'Protecting my investment.' I snapped and hung up. I pushed another coin into the machine and spun the dial again.

'Yeah?'

'Lantry here. Is the Colonel at home?'

'How should I know?' From the slurred voice and the heavy breathing I guessed who was at the other end of the line.

'Tell him I called, Stephan. Tell him that I've found his Norma. Tell him that I expect ten thousand dollars for finding her. Right?'

'Wait a minute.' Something seemed to have sobered him. 'What's that you say? You've found her?'

'That's right.'

'Where?'

'Where she's been all along.'

'Is she—?' He hesitated. 'Is she all right?'

'Why shouldn't she be?'

'I—' The silence which followed began to build up into something not quite nice. I cut it short.

'Just let the Colonel know, will you, Steve? I'm going back now.'

I slammed the receiver down and frowned at myself in the tiny mirror. Then I went out and caught a cab.

Though dark, it was still fairly early and the streets were full of people hurrying to get out of the cold. Underfoot the sidewalk was slippery with slush, already freezing, and I was glad to get inside the comparative warmth of police headquarters. I asked the desk sergeant where Captain Bresholm might be and he jerked a thumb towards his office. I knocked on the door and entered just in time to see him put down the phone. He grinned at me and waved me to a chair.

'Mike, it's good to see you. Smoke?'

'I'll use my own.' I lit a cigarette. 'Look, Bresholm, will you do something for me?'

'Sure, what is it?'

I told him.

He didn't like it, but he didn't shove the fact down my throat either. He thought about it, smoking his cigar and staring at me through the smoke. Finally, when I couldn't stand it much longer, he nodded.

'You think that it will work?'

'I don't know. There's a lot I don't know yet behind all this. Pug might be able to help us, but he's out of circulation. I'll have to do it the hard way and I'd like your co-operation.'

'If it was anyone else,' he said slowly, then shrugged. 'Hell, why not? If we can tie it up in a neat bundle, all the better. You sure that it will work?'

'No,' I said tiredly. 'I'm not sure. I only wish I was, but one thing I'm sure of. If there's a bunch of bulls stamping around, we'll get nowhere fast. I'd like to play it my way but I also want to stay in business, and I'm no hero. I've done my job, and I suppose that I could collect and forget it. I'd rather finish the thing right through.'

He didn't ask me why. If he had, I couldn't have told him. It was just one of those things, a clean finish and a clean start. No loose ends, nothing to worry about, no more dirt than necessary. And I had nothing to lose.

'Is Thornedyke mixed up in it?'

'I don't know but I think that he must be.' I looked at him. 'Why?'

'You tell me,' he said, and on one cheek a muscle began to twitch. I knew the signs and I knew that someone had been riding him. Politics, when coupled with the civil service, such as appointing the police commissioner, doesn't make for an efficient force. I leaned over the desk.

'Why don't you go in there and smash it up, Bresholm? Why let a dirty grafter like Thornedyke make a monkey out of you and the entire department? You could do it if you wanted to, you could grab his trigger-boys and put him where he'll give no more orders. Damn it, Bresholm, you shouldn't need me to tell you what needs doing.'

'I don't,' he said curtly.

'Then—'

'Cut it!' he snapped. 'Don't you think I know what you're getting at? You think I like things the way they are? But don't let this tin badge fool you, Lantry, I can be broken as easily as the rawest rookie on a beat. I know it and I daren't forget it.'

'Sorry.' I said it and I meant it. I was tired, run ragged, or I would never have needled him that way. He couldn't help it if he thought more of his wife and kids than a thing called 'honour.' And he could do more good where he was than pounding a beat.

I thought of something.

'Can I use your phone?'

'Sure, help yourself.'

'Can you tap the wire, record what's said?'

'Yes.' He looked surprised. 'You want me to?'

'Please.' I scribbled down a number. 'While you're doing it, find out where this is. Okay?'

He nodded and I dialled.

I could hear the phone ringing, one—two—three—then someone lifted the receiver and I waited for someone to speak. No one did so I did it for them.

'Hello? Is that Georgette?'

I heard a muffled sound as if someone was talking with a hand held over the receiver and not too well at that. Then a woman's voice echoed faintly in my ear.

'Who's that?'

'Mike, here. Mike Lantry.' I chuckled. 'I tried to contact you a while ago at the Purple Orchid, but they wouldn't connect us.'

'So you're John Weston.' She sounded relieved. 'I wondered who it could be.'

'That was me. Well, Georgette, did you get anything?'

She hesitated and I thought I heard someone say something.

'Hello, is anyone with you?'

'No.' She hesitated. 'Look, Mike, I can't talk now. Tell you what I'll do. Meet me at the corner of Tenth and Vine. There's a drugstore there; if you have to wait,

wait inside. Got it?'

'Sure, what time?'

'In a couple of hours, okay?'

'Sorry.' I listened to her intake of breath. 'I'm pretty busy. Can you make it an hour?'

'Sure.' I thought she sounded relieved. 'One hour from now, then. Corner of Tenth and Vine. Right?'

'Right. I'll be there.'

'Be seeing you.' She hesitated. 'Goodbye, shamus.' The phone went dead and I smiled at it, a long, slow smile.

Things were getting warm.

CHAPTER FOURTEEN

I arrived twenty minutes early and holed up in a doorway while I looked the place over. Tenth and Vine was in the slum area, not five blocks from where a dead woman stared from glassy eyes, and the general atmosphere was the same. The drugstore Georgette had mentioned threw bright light over the snow on the sidewalk. The other three corners were occupied by a junk shop, a second-hand clothing store, and a Chinese laundry. All had their windows covered by heavy shutters.

I let five minutes trickle into the great unknown, and then made up my mind. Standing out here would only get me cold feet, so I lit a cigarette, took a sharp walk around the block, and came towards the rendezvous from another direction. I walked past it, took another turn around the block, and walked back down a street, which gave me a clear view of both sides of the building. It was almost time now and Georgette, unless she were late, should be waiting inside the drugstore.

I slowed up as I neared the corner.

A light showed from the doorway of the junk shop, the red tip of a cigarette, and its glow threw into view a glimpse of sharp features, stooped shoulders, and a thin mouth. I crossed the street and went up to the doorway.

'Got a light, bud?'

He grunted and something gleamed in his hand. He stared at me, but my face was in shadow, the brim of my fedora pulled down over my eyes and my collar turned high around my neck. He hesitated for a second, then decided to give me what I'd asked for, holding out his cigarette for me to fire my own from its tip.

I laid the barrel of the Browning against the side of his head.

He grunted, sagging against the wall, and I caught him as he fell. I let him down lightly, hiding what I did with the bulk of my own body. He'd dropped the gun he'd been holding and I picked it up, broke it, and spilled out the shells. Then I dropped it into his lap and threw the bullets into the snow. Guns are heavy things, and I had enough to do carrying my own.

Then I crossed the street and entered the drugstore.

It was warm inside, with a sticky, unhealthy combination of smoke and cheap perfume, frying oil and burnt fat, onions and popcorn. A row of stools lined a long counter, a juke box thudded out something supposed to be music, and, if that wasn't noise enough, a pint-sized radio was turned on almost full blast.

The dispense counter held the usual assortment of tired toilet articles, household supplies, and dog-eared magazines. A phone booth stood in one corner, and the doors of the rest rooms stared at me like a couple of blind eyes.

I took a look at the people.

A bunch of adolescents jived to the tune of the juke box, stamping their feet and snapping their fingers like a gang of doped-up hepsters. A red-haired female, looking twice her age, giggled at a youthful escort and tried to pretend that she wasn't still attending school. An elderly man, his face a map of worry, dipped a sinker into his coffee and nibbled at the doughnut as if he hated the taste. Two men, well-dressed and poker-faced, stared into the back-mirror and let their coffee grow cold before them. A housewife, loaded with shopping, her false teeth making little clicking noises as she ate, gnawed at a sandwich.

No Georgette.

The soda jerk, a pockmarked man with a soiled apron and a heavy stubble on his receding chin, wiped his hands on a greasy apron and stepped forward to take my order.

'Coffee.' I dropped a nickel on the counter and reached for my cigarettes. Two people also reached for theirs, but I produced mine first. I snapped my lighter, lit the cigarette, then put the lighter into the left hand pocket of my gabardine. I left it there, hand and all, smoking and stirring my coffee with my right.

The two well-dressed men took no notice.

Five minutes trickled past, the door opened a couple of times, once to let the housewife out, and once to let a young girl in. Each time six eyes swivelled to the door and back to the mirror again.

No Georgette.

I crushed out my butt and rose from the stool. One of the poker-faced men stared at me, fumbled in his pocket and came up with a cigarette dangling from his lips.

'Light, mister?'

I jerked my head towards the counter.

'They sell matches. Buy some.'

He hadn't expected that. He stared at me, his eyes drifting from my scarred cheek to the notch in my ear, then he nodded.

I jumped all of five feet in a rearward direction.

The second man had left his stool and stood next to where I had been. He looked startled, even a little foolish, though there was nothing funny about the gun in his hand.

I shot him in the stomach using the Browning in my left-hand pocket.

He squealed and doubled up, the gun falling from his hand and making a clatter as it hit the floor. The other man said something, and took off in a movement which carried him behind the juke box and the gang of jivers. Fire spat towards me from the Luger he'd dragged from under his arm.

I ducked, letting my right hand do its work, and tried for a clear shot. He didn't worry about waiting for that, and the roar of the Luger mingled with the screams and yells of the customers as they fought their way out of the drugstore and into the street.

I rolled as lead chipped fragments from the terrazzo

floor, and magazines cascaded around me as I bumped into the magazine stand. I triggered three times, sending lead into the red and chromium shape of the juke box, and it fell silent with a tinny rattle. The gunsel ducked. I clawed my way free from the hampering papers and structure of the magazine stand, sent three more shots towards where the gunner waited to kill me, and took a flying leap over the counter.

The soda-jerk gibbered at me, the carving knife in his hand trembling as he tried to stick it into my side. I knocked it from his hand, ran the full length of the counter, and peered around the far end.

I saw a man's back, the heel of a shoe and a tense face as he guessed what was happening and turned to face me. I saw the Luger in his hand rise and level itself, but I didn't give him time to blow me apart. I squeezed the trigger once.

Once was enough.

I rose and stared down at him, at the small, neat, black-edged hole between his eyes. I didn't want to see the back of his head, but I could guess what it was like. A 9mm. slug is no toy and it plays for keeps.

I put my left hand on the counter, vaulted over it, and took a quick look round.

The place was a mess.

Glass and plastic had spilled from the ruined juke box. The floor was covered with magazines from the rack, and smashed crockery littered the floor. The blood didn't help either.

The soda-jerk peeped over the counter, saw my gun,

and turned white. I grinned at him and put it away. It made him feel a little better, not much, but a little, and he lost some of his green tinge.

I didn't say anything and he, after two false starts, decided to follow my example. The wounded man whimpered as he clutched at his perforated stomach, writhing like a half-squashed insect as he stared up at me with pain-glazed eyes. I looked down at him, feeling no pity, no remorse, no nothing. He would have killed me if I hadn't got him first.

It was as simple as that.

Outside the night air seemed fresh and clean after the assorted smells of the drugstore. A few men hung around the edge of light thrown from the windows, staring with wide eyes and thrilling to the near-touch of danger. None of them said anything to me, and I didn't want to talk to them. I ignored them, feeling safe now that I had got the two goons inside, and knowing that I'd already settled the outside man, the one who would have got me had the other two failed.

It had been a nice, neat, well-laid trap.

I didn't realise just how well-laid.

I sent my legs in long strides over the frozen slush, glancing at my watch and trying to make up for lost time. From a long way away, somewhere behind me, the shrill note of a siren began to torture the air as the cops came to the scene of the fray.

I shrugged, putting distance between myself and them, letting others worry about the immediate explanations.

I never even heard the car.

It came like a long, black ghost, its engine cut and its own momentum carrying it along the street as it swept up behind me. Frozen snow crunched beneath the wheels making a small, forlorn little sound, and attracted by that sound, I turned just in time.

A face peered at me from the rear seat. A snarling, swollen face, ugly and with sticking plaster pasted over the nose. Below the face snouted the squat muzzle of a Thompson.

I flung myself down as the sub-machine gun chattered a rasping invitation to hell, rolling as lead stabbed towards me, feeling the cold chill of the snow against my face and feeling the burn as something drilled into my left arm.

Desperately I tugged at the holstered Browning, jerking it free as I rolled towards the centre of the road, the frozen slush clawing at my face. The engine of the car roared into life and the back wheels spun, showering me with ice-spray and almost blinding me.

I squeezed the trigger.

I didn't try any fancy shooting. I didn't try to puncture a tyre or anything like that. I just lifted the muzzle and poured the contents of the magazine into the body of the car, swinging the gun so as to traverse the interior and hoping that I'd hit warm flesh as well as cold metal.

I was lucky.

I heard the driver scream as hot lead explored his vitals and the big car jerked as his dying foot trod on the gas. It skidded, slewed, and rammed hard against a lamp-post. Fire blossomed from it, some of my shots must have hit the gas tank, because flames began to spread all around the wrecked vehicle.

I dragged myself to my feet and holstered the empty gun. I twisted and managed to get the spare Browning from my left-hand pocket. Holding it, I walked towards the leaping pyre, feeling the heat of the burning gasoline warm against the skin of my face and hands.

A man scrambled from the rear seat. A man with a snarling mouth and badly bruised face. He still held the Thompson and, as he saw me, he said something and lifted the gun.

'You dirty shamus,' screamed Lefty. 'I'll—'

I shot him in the chest.

The impact of the slug knocked him off balance, threw him backwards into the burning car, and I heard him scream as he felt the bite of the flames. He couldn't have felt them long, though, because he only screamed the once, and then it was silent aside from the crackling of the fire.

I watched it for a while, letting it warm me, and feeling pain and life return to my injured arm. Then I moved away.

I felt sick, a little dizzy, and more than a little tired.

I wanted a drink, a smoke, a bath. I wanted a week of lying in the sun, a month of good food, a year of sleep. But I had work to do and those things had to wait.

I headed towards 354 Green Street, where a dead woman waited for me to keep her company.

CHAPTER FIFTEEN

The apartment was just as I'd left it. Darker, colder, a little more haunted, but that might have been my imagination.

I let the door swing softly shut behind me then, gun in hand, I made a quick tour just in case. I found what I'd expected to find. Nothing.

Drawing the heavy drapes I switched on the lights, made sure that the door was locked, and found the bottle of rye I'd left to keep the dead woman company. I took a quick drink straight from the bottle, took another from a glass, and then set to work to assess my damage.

It wasn't as bad as I'd thought. The tommy-gun slug had ripped through the fleshy part of my upper arm but had missed the bone and come out clean. I stripped off my shirt, tore off the tail, and with water from the kitchen, washed off the blood and bandaged it as well as I could. Messing around with it made it hurt even more than before, so I took time out to have some more rye before getting dressed again.

It was when I looked at the gabardine that I realised how lucky I'd been.

The spray of shots from the machine gun must have followed me as I rolled, and providence, or maybe a clean life, or even my Guardian Angel had been working overtime. It was full of holes, ripped, torn, and, as a garment fit for wear it was useless. Still, it was all I had and it was cold, and so I put it on and tried to forget what I must look like. I moved through the apartment doing what I had to do, setting empty bottles where they would do the most good, beneath the window, in front of the door, setting a row just below the opening to the fire escape, and putting a couple on the escape itself.

Going back into the main room I drew up a chair, set the bedside table close to it, put the bottle on the table, and took a look round. I remembered something else, and made sure that the gun under my arm was the one with the shells in it. The other gun, the empty one, I put beside the bottle. I made a couple of telephone calls, listened to the striking of a clock somewhere in the city then, drawing back the drapes, I turned off the lights, sat down, and waited.

It was a hell of a wait.

I couldn't smoke and I couldn't move around. All I could do was to nibble at the rye and think. I did plenty of that.

I thought of a dead woman and what she had done and what had been done to her. I imagined her alive and well, lissome and graceful, vibrant and eager, her lips ripe for kissing and her face for smiling. A woman, one of a million, and yet, to herself, the most important thing there ever was or could be. I imagined her as she was, cold, twisted, dead, gone forever.

I sighed as I thought of the dead.

I thought of the living, of a young man who had taken to worshiping a bottle and what its contents could do for him. Of an old man and what he had tried to do. Of a girl and the way she had looked at me. I thought of Bresholm, and Thornedyke, and Pug lying in hospital well out of it all.

I thought of Constance, and thought of her some more.

And I sighed as I thought of the living.

I reached for the bottle and tried to keep warm. Far away the same clock struck and struck again and then again. Around me the apartment grew as frigid as an icebox, and the odour of the dead mingled with the stale scent of dust and the raw scent of the rye. I waited, and my nerves grew taut and as brittle as glass.

The shrill of the doorbell almost made me jump out of my skin.

I sat there, breathing through my open mouth, one hand resting on the switch of the table-lamp, the other gripping the butt of my gun. I didn't move.

The buzzer sounded again, throbbing through the night like a call for help, shrilling with quick, short bursts as though whoever it was was getting tired and impatient and wanted in. It stopped and I could hear the sound of heavy breathing from outside the door The buzzer sounded again, quick and sharp, and then came the knocking, hard, violent, making the door tremble in its frame.

I rose from the chair, walked across to it, tucked my gun beneath my left arm, and with my right hand, twisted the knob. As it opened I stepped to one side, the Browning heavy in my fist.

Stephan looked at me, one hand still raised as though to knock again, and the hall-light streaming over his shoulder revealed my face and the gun in my hand. I jerked the weapon.

'Come inside.'

He nodded and I shut the door behind him. I switched on the lights and stared at him.

'Well?'

'Where is she?' He looked at the apartment, his face all eyes.

'Don't you know?' I leaned against the wall, the gun back in its resting place, and slipped a cigarette between my lips. I lit it, dragging gratefully at the blue smoke, watching him as he moved around the dirty room. I watched him as he stared towards the folded-back bed, then he saw the bottle and he reached for it, tilted it, and put it down again almost empty.

'You know where she is, don't you, Stephan?' I didn't make it a question.

'I thought you said that you did.'

'I didn't tell you this address. I didn't tell you anything but that I'd found her. You filled in the rest. You knew where to come because you've been here before.' I stepped close to him and stared into his eyes.

'Well, Stephan? Why don't you make sure?'

'I don't know what you mean.' He was trembling now and his hand shook as he reached for the bottle. I knocked it away.

'Don't you, Stephan?' I pushed him and he staggered back against the wall. 'I'll show you what I mean.'

The catch twisted easily in my hand and the bed made a soft, sighing sound as it swung from the wall. I didn't look towards the bed. I didn't have to. I'd seen it before. I looked at Stephan's face, at his expression as he stared at what I'd revealed.

'God!' It was a prayer the way he said it. 'She's dead!'

'Yeah.' I sucked at my cigarette. 'Surprised?'

'You think that I killed her?' He looked at me with a kind of desperate frenzy. 'You fool! I couldn't have killed her. I loved her! Understand? I was crazy about her.'

'"Each man kills the thing he loves",' I quoted, and even to me the words sounded trite. 'You were in love with her. but she chose to marry your father. You knew that she was here. You maybe argued with her but, being what she was, she wouldn't chance losing a certain fortune for a drunken sot. You couldn't have her, so you killed her.' I blew smoke towards him. 'Finished. Case solved. You burn at midnight.'

'No.' He wiped his face with the flat of his hand and turned away from the bed. This time when he reached for the bottle I didn't stop him. 'I didn't kill her, Lantry. I loved her, yes. I wanted her to run away with me, yes. But I didn't kill her.'

I shrugged and concentrated on my cigarette.

'I didn't kill her,' he repeated. 'I couldn't have done.'

'Why not?' I was deliberately cynical. 'Your old man grabbed her away from you and they both enjoyed the joke. You were probably drunk and had a fight. You thought it smart to shut her up in the bed. Maybe you didn't know she was still alive or maybe you did, but she didn't stay that way long. She was upside down, trapped, without enough air to breath. So she died the hard way all alone in her temporary coffin.' I looked at him. 'Or did you think to cop a plea of unintentional murder?'

'For God's sake, Lantry!' He hid his face between his hands and I saw his shoulders heave. I didn't give him any pity.

'You knew where she was without my telling you. You had the motive, the opportunity, and her death would have put money in your pocket. It's no good, Stephan. You're all washed up. Why don't you confess and get it over with?'

'No.' He stared at me and his eyes reminded me of an animal I'd once seen at the Bronx Zoo. Trapped, helpless, asking for mercy, and not finding it anywhere.

'You've got it all wrong.'

'Well?'

'I've been here before, not inside the apartment, but to the door. She didn't know that, she thought that I was downstairs, but I'd followed her and—'

'Take it from the beginning.' I suggested.

'Yes. Well, it was this way. She came to me and asked me to help her. She knew how I felt about her, but there was nothing like you suggest. She wanted me to drive her here and I did. I followed her up the stairs and saw her enter this apartment. Someone let her in, a man, I think, but I wasn't sure. I waited. I waited a long time but she never came out. So I drove back home.'

'That was on the night she vanished?'

'Yes.'

'Why didn't you tell me all this before?'

'I didn't think that she'd like it?' He looked at me defiantly and I let it pass.

'Was she in any trouble at home? Money or anything like that?'

'I wouldn't know.'

'Yes, you would,' I snapped. 'You were in love with her and she must have had some feeling for you. You used to run around together, remember? Did she ever ask you for any money?'

I read my answer in his eyes.

'So she did.' I glared at him. 'If you'd have told me all this before— Hell! What's the use? You're still the patsy though. You're the only one who, on your own admission, could have killed her.'

'But I didn't.' His face altered as he thought about it. 'Wait a minute! There's someone else!' He stared hopefully at me. 'She said something coming down in the car. I never thought about it at the time but—'

I got to him just in time. The glass warned me, the bottles I'd spread around for just this emergency, and as I heard one topple over with a dull thud, I was already moving. I knocked Stephan to the floor and dived after him just as a gun sent lead whining towards us.

It hammered again, and I felt splinters from the floor rip my cheek. Then I had the Browning in my hand and was triggering lead towards the kitchen.

Someone yelled, glass splintered in a thousand crystalline tinklings, and silence replaced the roar of exploding cartridges. Stephan moaned, blood oozing from a scalp wound and I spared him a second to make sure that he was still alive. He was and I headed towards the kitchen.

Bottles fell away from beneath my feet. I tripped and grabbed at the window-sill to save myself and felt glass cut my palm. I ignored it, eeling through the window and out on to the rusty fire-escape.

Fire winked at me from halfway down and lead whined as it bounced off the metal just above my head. I snapped a shot towards it without any real hope of hitting anything, then, sweating with the pain from my wrenched arm, I started down the stairs as if all the dogs of Hell were snapping at my heels.

He was waiting for me at the bottom.

I guessed it and hung back, letting my eyes probe the darkness and shadows as I crouched back against the wall. The area was dimly lighted by the reflected light of the street lamps, and pools of thick shadow lay everywhere. From somewhere in the distance the sirens of a police car moved rapidly towards us. Cops called by some scared neighbour. The sound frightened the man in the shadows and I heard him curse from a dimly seen corner.

I triggered three shots in that direction and got two back in exchange. Neither of them did any harm, but I let out a yell and jumped the last ten feet to the floor, hitting hard and rolling to one side, coming up with my gun at the ready. He could have got me then. He could have remained cool and blasted me as I landed, before I'd got my balance or could see what was going on. But he didn't. Maybe he thought that he'd hit me. Maybe he was scared of the noise of the sirens. But fear had closed around him and panic had him by the throat.

He ran.

I ran after him, watching his silhouette against the brightly lit street. I watched him, taking my time, and when I lifted the Browning it was just as though I was shooting clay-pipes at a carnival range.

I didn't kill him. That would have been too easy, too merciful, too generous a gesture for all that he'd done. Anyway, I'd promised to deliver him ready for the electric chair. So I shot his legs out from under him and sent him rolling into the gutter where he belonged.

He screamed as he fell, twisting to bring his own gun into play, so I had to smash his shoulder in sheer self-defence before walking up to stare down into his face.

He snarled at me, no longer neat, no longer well-groomed, and his eyes filled with hate as they focused on me.

'Good-evening, Mr. Wendle,' I said. And laughed as he tried to spit in my face.

CHAPTER SIXTEEN

The police had arrived, and the ambulance had come, and gone and the newspapermen had flashed their cameras and grabbed what they could. I sat in a police car, shivering, my arm burning, and generally felt like all hell. Bresholm came out of the building, nodded to a photog, then slipped into the car with me. He passed me a bottle and I sniffed at it. Scotch, the best, and I thanked him with my eyes as I warmed my interior.

'Well?' he said quietly. 'It almost went wrong, didn't it?'

'It did.' I grinned as Constance, her face flushed and her eyes eager, crowded into the car with us. She helped herself to a drink, lit two cigarettes, and stuck one in my mouth.

'A scoop,' she said happily. 'Mike, I could kiss you!'

'Don't let me stop you,' said Bresholm. 'But can't you leave it till later?'

'Thanks,' I said dryly, and consoled myself with more of the Scotch.

'Spill it, Mike,' he said evenly. 'All of it. What happened?'

'Our little trap almost blew up in my face,' I said. 'Wendle killed Mrs. Geeson. I thought it had to be someone close to her, but I didn't think of the lawyer. Now that I know he did it, the rest all fits in.'

'Blackmail?' Bresholm raised his eyebrows.

'Right in one, but a little more involved than that. As I suspected, Mrs. Geeson hadn't been born Mona Hartridge. She was originally known as Rhoda Fleming and, while using that name, met and married a man. We can soon find out who it was, but my guess is that she married Thornedyke.'

'The gambler?' Constance didn't seem to want to believe it. 'But Mike, he wouldn't let her commit bigamy.'

'For ten million dollars, Thornedyke would do anything,' I said bitterly 'He's that kind of a rat.' I looked at Bresholm. 'Did you clear up the mess?'

'Yes. The man you only wounded is ready to talk. Thornedyke hired him, of course, and the phone message came from the Purple Orchid. Thornedyke himself doesn't enter into it, but we can get him just the same. Conspiring to commit a felony,' he explained. 'The dame Georgette is ready to talk. Her testimony and that of the gunsel should persuade the District Attorney that he's got a case. At least,' Bresholm said grimly, 'it had better.'

'If it doesn't the *Tribune* will flay him,' said Constance happily. 'Thanks for phoning. Mike, we got pics and everything and I'll get a bonus.'

'Forget it.' I winced as I moved my damaged wing.

'When Thornedyke found out that Norma was running around with Stephan, he didn't like it and I guess that it was about then he tied the nuptial knot. The Colonel didn't know that and, to save his son from making a fool of himself, he offered the girl his heart and hand and fortune. Naturally, he had her checked and that is where Wendle got his bright idea.

'He learned that she was married but, at the same time, he saw a way to make an easy dollar. He persuaded her to fake her identification—in fact, she merely took Georgette's original name—and go through the ceremony. Thornedyke, her legal husband, had his own ideas. He was playing for the jackpot, the entire works, and my guess is that it was only a matter of time before he bumped off the Colonel, let Norma collect, and then stepped in to claim the booty.' I sucked down some smoke to kill the taste in my mouth.

'A nice, neat, fool-proof scheme. Only it didn't work out just the way he wanted it to.'

'I still can't understand how any man would let his wife do that,' complained Constance. 'He must have had some feeling for her.'

'Not in the way you're thinking,' I said. 'Thornedyke and Norma were man and wife only on paper. I doubt if they had ever really lived together. I'm guessing, don't forget, maybe it wasn't Thornedyke at all, maybe it was some heel who she'd fallen for years ago and who had walked out on her. The point is that Thornedyke knew about it and wouldn't let her divorce whoever it was until it was too late. She'd married the Colonel by then and while he could hold her bigamy over her head, she had to play it his way. Add Wendle to the mess and you get a nice, sweet set-up. Sweet that is, for them; Norma didn't think it so hot.'

'She kicked?'

'And hard.' I paused, smoking and getting my thoughts in order. 'I don't know all the ins and outs; that can come later when we have time to check. But this is what I think happened. Wendle knew of the earlier marriage. He put the pressure on and had her send him money to an accommodation address, the Green Street apartment. Harmond had the job of posting the letters and, finally, when she grew desperate, he took her wristwatch, some keepsake she'd had for years, and hocked that too. Finally, she took her jewels and tried to buy Wendle off. It didn't work.'

'He killed her.' Bresholm nodded. 'I can see that. She threatened to expose him, of course.'

'Maybe.'

'But if Thornedyke was protecting her, then why didn't he rub the lawyer out?' Constance thoughtfully lit a fresh cigarette. 'It seems the obvious thing to do.'

'I thought of that,' I said, 'and this is how I see it: Wendle was a lawyer and would have protected himself. We'll probably find that he left letters or something to be opened if he was found dead, or vanished, or didn't report in at regular intervals. Thornedyke must have known this and, more important, Thornedyke needed Wendle more than Wendle needed Thornedyke. Wendle would be the one to probate the will. He could make it smooth or he could make it hard. He could blow the entire scheme with a word and, if he wasn't around to handle things, someone else might check and discover the earlier marriage. Result, no money, no nothing. It was safer to keep Wendle alive.'

'And the blackmail?'

'Strictly Wendle's idea. He must be pressed for cash, if he wasn't he would have remained honest in the first place. He couldn't wait, maybe he was fixing the books or something, and he wanted to get what he could as soon as he could. So he applied pressure. Norma, terrified at losing her chance of a decent life, tried to buy him off. Result—end of Norma.'

'So you found the body and decided to set a trap.'

'A trap that almost didn't work. I fixed it with Bresholm to stand by, but when Stephan walked in, he thought that it was all over. Wendle crawled up the fire escape; he knew that Norma was dead, but Stephan thought that she was still alive. The poor sucker was still in love with her and wanted to see her.' I looked at Bresholm. 'Incidentally, there should have been an officer on that fire-escape.'

'There was,' he said shortly. 'Wendle sapped him.'

'Anyway, he listened in and decided to make a clean sweep of it. Norma must have told Stephan what was going on when he drove her down. That's why no one knew anything about her leaving the house, Stephan wasn't supposed to drive.'

'And Harmond?' Bresholm seemed satisfied.

'Wendle. He must have had an idea that the old

man knew too much. He followed him and rubbed him out. At that he was lucky, Pug almost caught him, but he managed to get into his car and put Pug where he couldn't do any harm. Wendle must have phoned Thornedyke too to warn him that I was getting nosey. Or maybe having me beat up was Thornedyke's own idea. It doesn't matter now anyway.'

I dropped my hand on to the latch and opened the door of the car.

'Where are you going?' Bresholm stared at me. 'I'll take you home.'

'Take Constance home,' I said. 'I'm going for a walk.'

He didn't argue. Constance tried to, but he shut her up and I was grateful for him for doing it. Walking slowly down the street, I had time to think of what I had said.

Logical?

Well, perhaps. Wendle had killed the missing woman. Thornedyke had been after the Geeson fortune. Norma had wanted to break loose and make another start.

No need to go into details about how Stephan had known more than he said, or about how the Colonel hadn't wanted the police because he was afraid that one or both of his own children might have been responsible. Or about how Marvin was terrified I would find out something harmful to the family. Or why Susan gambled away a small fortune at the Purple Orchid.

It didn't matter now. Nothing mattered. The case was over.

Almost.

The car drew up beside me with a sigh of brakes, and the rear door swung open with mute invitation. I climbed in. It was warm, snug, and smelled of polished leather and good cigars. The Colonel was there, and Susan, and between the front and back of the car the division which shut off the driver had been lowered. Marvin turned and smiled and I smiled back.

'Well?' The Colonel was testy. 'What did you tell them?'

'The minimum. Wendle killed her and Harmond. Why?'

'Nothing.' He breathed a deep sigh of relief. 'I thought—'

'You thought that Stephan had killed her. Marvin thought so too; he would know that a car had been used that night and he would know who drove it. Susan thought the same, so she deliberately threw some money towards Thornedyke via the gambling tables to keep him quiet. Did he ask for it or did you offer it?'

'He hinted something,' said the Colonel quietly. 'I didn't know what to do' His hand fell and gripped Susan's fingers. 'Stephan is almost all I have.'

'Stephan is all right,' I said 'When he gets over that knock on the head, send him away for a cure and start him over again. He took it hard, but that was your fault. He loved his mother and didn't like you setting up a cheap imitation in her place.' I stopped his protests. 'I know. You thought that it would be for his own good. Colonel, one day you'll learn that you just can't do things for people's own good. They have to do it their way or it doesn't count.'

'You mean well,' he said, still stiff, 'but—'

'But you think I ought to keep my big mouth shut.' I shrugged. 'Maybe I should, but what else do you expect when you hire a private eye? Did you want me to sit on my tail and say nothing, do nothing? And what did you think I was going to do when everyone tried to deny every fact in the world? You can't cover up murder, Colonel, not even when you think that it's been done by your own son. What's the point in employing someone to do a job if you refuse to help him do it?'

He didn't answer and I didn't blame him.

'Sorry. Maybe I shouldn't talk like that but I've had a hell of a time. When I think of the difference a little help would have made—'

'I'm sorry,' he said, and for him it was a big admission. 'I made a mistake, I realise that now, but how was I to know that you were to be trusted?'

'You didn't know,' I said. 'That's the trouble with this racket. People need help, but they are afraid that in getting out of it they will get in more.' I grinned at him. 'Don't get me wrong, most of the private eyes are honest enough, but there are even more who will find out what they can, and pass it on to someone who will try to make a little extra money on the side. Forget it.'

'I won't forget it,' he said quietly. Paper rustled and in the roof-light I could see the rich green of hundred dollar bills.

'Ten thousand dollars was the agreed fee, Mr.

Lantry.' He passed it to me and I took it. Why not? It was money fairly earned.

'Thank you, Colonel.'

'This is for your discretion.' He held out more money and I shook my head.

'No.'

'No? Why not?'

'You set a price and I agreed to it.' I felt too tired to explain that even a man who goes to work with a gun under his arm can have ethics. 'But there is something you can do for me.'

'Anything.'

'Send a thousand dollars to a girl named Georgette. Bresholm has her in protective custody and will pass it on to her.'

'Certainly, may I ask why?'

'She saved my life.'

No need to tell him how she had tipped me off that I was heading for trouble. No one says 'good-bye' to a person they expect to meet within the hour. Not a girl like that, anyway, and the last two words she had spoken over the telephone had given me the tip-off. I reached for the door handle.

'May I drive you home, Mr. Lantry?'

'No thank you.' I grinned at him, then at Susan. I winked.

'Marvin is crazy about you,' I said. 'He even tried to beat me up a couple of times because he thought that I might discover something to hurt you. Probably he's too shy to tell you himself, so you can take it as words from a friend.'

She blushed and, from what I could see, Marvin was blushing too. The Colonel stared at me, then at his daughter, then held out his hand.

'Thank you again, Mr. Lantry.'

'Make it Mike.'

'Thank you, Mike. I know a lot of people and I know now that you are to be trusted. Don't be surprised if you get quite a few cases soon.' He smiled, a friendly smile. 'I don't think that all of them will be as hectic as this one was.'

I stepped out of the car then and watched it drive away.

People. They're all the same. They employ a man to clean up their trouble and then get scared because he may find out too much. So they lie and cheat and deny and make a hard job even harder for everyone, including themselves.

But I felt good as I stared after the car.

The Colonel had ten million dollars and he had friends. Wealthy people are always in trouble of one sort or another, and his recommendation would go a long way to putting me where I wanted to get. To the top, to the place where my agency would be the biggest and best.

And if I had a little trouble getting there, well, what of it?

Trouble was my business.

ABOUT THE AUTHOR

English writer **E. C. TUBB** is internationally known, having been translated into more than a dozen languages. In a sixty-year writing career he published over 120 novels, and more than 200 science fiction short stories in such magazines as *Astounding/Analog*, *Authentic*, *Fantasy Adventures*, *Galaxy*, *Nebula*, *New Worlds*, *Science Fantasy*, and *Vision of Tomorrow*.

Tubb's early science fiction novels were exciting adventure stories, written in the prevailing fashion of the early 1950s. Yet, from his very first novel, his work was characterized at all times by a sense of plausibility, logic, and human insight. These qualities were even more evident in his short stories, which were frequently anthologized.

By 1956 his output included adventure, detective stories, and westerns, but he remained best known for his numerous science fiction novels, of which *Alien Dust* (1955) and *The Space Born* (1956) were acknowledged classics. Tubb became famous for his long-running "Dumarest of Terra" series of novels, the galaxy-spanning saga of Earl Dumarest and his search to find his way back across the stars to the legendary lost planet where he was born—Earth. They eventually spanned thirty-three titles, the final one, *Child of Earth*, appearing in November 2008. Equally well known were his *Space 1999* TV novelizations, and his "Cap Kennedy" novels. Some of his finest SF short stories were collected in *The Best Science Fiction of E. C. Tubb* (Wildside, 2003). Tubb continued to write dynamic science fiction novels right up to his death in October, 2010.

www.ingramcontent.com/pod-product-compliance
Lightning Source LLC
Chambersburg PA
CBHW031424250626
47155CB00004B/1622